Pieces of Dreams

Rafael —
Don't wait!
make your dream
come true.
Kinopenolti!
Elvira LA

Elvira Ledesma Aguayo

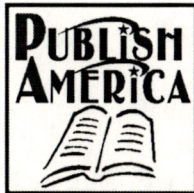

PUBLISH AMERICA

PublishAmerica
Baltimore

ISBN: 1-4241-6712-4
PUBLISHED BY PUBLISHAMERICA, LLLP
www.publishamerica.com
Baltimore

Printed in the United States of America

I dedicate this book to my two mothers, Dorita Lerma Ledesma and Beatriz Espinosa Aguayo, who smile down on me and mine from heaven, and to my father, Margarito Escobedo Ledesma.

Many people helped and encouraged me along the way: my parents, my brothers and sisters. My two daughters, Maricruz and Marta offered not only encouragement but also very helpful critique when asked. My husband Jesse gave me total support and encouragement; he even drew a picture of the main character in her blue wedding dress. I had it taped to the wall above my computer as I wrote her story.

My colleague and friend Isabel Corona has offered support, as has my good friend Virginia (Ginny) Rivas Champion.

I would also like to thank Dr. James Evans, professor at University of Texas-Pan American in Edinburg. I was working on my MA and enrolled in his class on the Southwest in American Literature. He required grad students to write a first or last chapter of a novel set in the American Southwest, and I did. It grew into this novel, *Pieces of Dreams*. It is not the first or last chapter, but it is in there.

Many others have read this manuscript and encouraged me to get it published. Thank you all for your support.

ONE

The old man stood on the mountain, looking down on his village. He breathed deeply of the cool mountain air and began his descent. He walked and walked yet got no closer to his home. A shadow passed over him, over the village. He tried to yell out a warning, but no sound escaped him. The air became dark, suffocating. He fell to his knees, gasping for breath. He struggled against the enveloping darkness with limbs that were too heavy to lift.

Suddenly a soothing brilliance surrounded him, and he rose above the shadow. He was floating up, up…He looked down towards the place that had been his village and saw only rubble.

On his right was a woman clothed in rose and turquoise. He recognized her as the Lady of his dreams, the one who had shown him the way for his people many times. Her face held deep suffering suffused with a wondrous peace. She opened her arms and he took a hesitant step toward her, then turned again to his village. He looked into her face, pleading. She smiled, stooped down, and picked up a blue stone. She caressed the stone, held it close to her breast for a moment and handed it to him, motioning that he should roll it down the mountain to the valley below. He held the stone to his heart for a moment then placed it gently on the ground and gave it a push.

It rolled gently at first. Then, gathering speed, it went past the ruined village, and even past the city at the base of the mountain. Bits of the shadow still clung to it, but *the stone was whole, and it was still moving. The old man turned and walked into the woman's embrace. And as she covered him with her turquoise cape, he experienced a peace he had never felt before.*

1

December 1944

María Dolores awoke before sunrise. It was December 12, the feast day of the Virgen de Guadalupe, but they would have no celebration in the village. She sat up, blessed herself in the name of the Father and of the Son and of the Holy Spirit, walked to the washbowl and rinsed the sleep out of her face. She tried for a moment to remember the dream she'd had, but couldn't quite grasp it. She stoked the embers of the cooking fire. She took cornmeal and lightly toasted it in the pot, then added some goat's milk and honey to make *atole*. When the mixture was simmering, she added a bit of cinnamon for flavor. As she stirred the cereal, she prayed that this meal bring nourishment and healing to her ailing grandfather. She took the clay pot off the fire and set it aside to cool as she dressed.

In honor of the Virgin she wore the pale blue dress she had first worn on her wedding day, exactly three months earlier, on the fourteenth anniversary of her birth. Two weeks after the ceremony, the first of the villagers had fallen ill and died. The plague was highly contagious. At first one by one, then by families, the villagers had died. Her husband and both her parents had succumbed just five days ago. María Dolores had nursed them, as they had helped nurse others in the village. She had no time to mourn, for now her grandfather Teoxihuitl, baptized Diego, was ill, too. She left her hut and headed next door to see him.

The girl hesitated before entering her grandfather's hut. Sister Consuelo, the catechist, saw her at the entrance and came out of the hut. The old man had not slept well, she told the girl. At one point he must have been dreaming, for he had struggled and moaned about a shadow and the light. Then he had awakened briefly, smiling peacefully, and had just now dozed off again. The nun touched the girl's chin and lifted the face. In the sounds of the native language, she told her that there was not much time left. She walked off in the direction of the stream.

María Dolores blessed herself and slipped in quietly, so as not to disturb her grandfather, but he was awake and waiting for her.

"Yolihuani," he whispered, speaking their native Nahuatl, using her Indian name. "My time has come. Tata Dios, Father God, has given me many years, more than I could have wished for."

"Nonsense, Grandfather," she replied. She busied herself with the cereal, gently stirring it.

But the grandfather insisted that she must listen, for his time was short and he had to instruct her, to offer his protection. He knew that his granddaughter would not die with the village, that her destiny lay elsewhere.

María Dolores put down the pot and knelt beside him. She looked around at the walls of the hut. Her eyes fell on the ojo de Dios above her grandfather's bed. It had a small crucifix attached to it, showing that the family had been converted to Christianity. A small picture of Our Lady of Guadalupe hung beside it. She silently begged the Virgin to give her grandfather more time.

Don Diego smiled at his granddaughter. "Don't ask the Lady to do the impossible, *nocihuanton*, my little girl. I am ready to go to Tata Dios. I want to see your grandmother and your mother and father. But I have to tell you what I want for you, Yolihuani. You must go down, all the way into Tequila. To the house of *toteotzin*. The priest will help you. I have sent a message to Padre Santiago. He will be expecting you. You go there, and he will advise you and help you make your way. Soon, there will be nothing left of the village. Those who remain with life will scatter to the four winds. You must be strong and make a life for yourself. Go forward always; do not look back. Promise me that you will do this."

María Dolores, weeping now, sobbed quietly. "Tata, do not speak of these things. I will take care of you and you will get better. I do not want to go to the city. I want to be here, with you. I want…"

"Yolihuani, *nic nequil*. I want it so. You will do as I tell you. I must go, and you must do what you can to have a better life. Life is a long walk home, as you well know. It is time for you to walk again. The village was good in its time, but it cannot give you a life after I am gone. You must be strong, and you must go forward." He took the gold chain with the medal of Our Lady off his neck and placed it on hers. "Now come close, that I may give you my blessing." He made the sign of the cross, touching her forehead, her chest, and both shoulders, and whispered, "*Ximopanolti*. Go safely." He closed his eyes as if to sleep, then opened them and looked up, past her left shoulder. He raised his arm in greeting. "*Cualli tlanezi, nocihuapili*. Good morning, my Lady."

María Dolores cried out, "Tata! Don't leave me!" and the few villagers who were left rushed into the hut. Sister Consuelo and Sister Juana took her outside to allow the men to prepare the body for burial. The preparations were done quickly. The villagers buried Don Diego, using the prayers that the padrecitos had taught them for the burial rites. That same night they began the novena of rosaries for the repose of his soul. Throughout the mourning time, Maria Dolores held herself in check. She asked the Lady for the strength to meet the pain with calm, and she knew her grandfather would have been proud of her.

Nine days later, Maria Dolores packed her belongings: two dresses, the small clay pot that her mother had given her as a wedding present, the ojo de Dios with the crucifix on it, and the picture of the Lady from her grandfather's hut. She walked out of the village that had been her world, and made her way down the mountain to the city.

2

Father Santiago let out a deep sigh when he saw her at his doorstep. She did not look like the happy little girl who always accompanied her grandfather when they met in the village, or even like the young woman who had been among the brides at the marriage ceremony he held in the village just over three months ago. She had always been full of life, spirited. Yolihuani, he learned from her mother when they baptized her, meant 'source of life.' He had wanted to respect the appropriateness of that, so he had baptized her Maria Dolores; it was the Marian name that most closely sounded like her Indian name.

Her presence could only mean that Don Diego had succumbed to the influenza. The old man had sent word just last week, when his daughter and son-in-law had died, asking the priest to look after the girl if it came to that. Perhaps if someone else looked at her, they would think she looked serene, but he knew her better than that. Indeed, she looked as if she would soon fall apart. He looked into her eyes. Today, they were without light. He put his hand on her shoulder and murmuring words of consolation, gave her permission to cry.

"Oh, child, let it out. You need a good cry. Have you been holding it in all this time? Here, Maria Dolores, Yolihuani, sit here and let it out." He showed her to the most comfortable chair in his office and gave her his handkerchief.

Feeling safe in the priest's presence, Maria Dolores cried for the first time since the illness had struck her village. Back then, there had been no time to cry. There had only been time to bury the dead and tend to the sick. Now she could mourn for her parents, her husband, her grandfather, and her way of life. As she accepted the handkerchief from Padre Santiago, she let roll the tears that had been biding their time. Then a low moan escaped from the very center of her being, and she began to sob, almost silently, betrayed only by the shaking of her shoulders, the periodic intake of breath. After a quarter of an hour, the sobbing subsided. Tears stained her face as she faced the priest again.

"My grandfather said I must go forward always. His last word to me was Ximopanolti. Then he greeted the Lady, and went with her. I know that he went safely. He told me that you would help, that I must leave the place that had been our home. I will do what you say, Father."

When she had finished, he said, "Don Diego was right. You will have a new life here." He called Tencha, the housekeeper, and asked her to see to the girl. Tencha took Maria Dolores back through the kitchen and the patio to the servants' quarters. As she did so, she appraised the girl.

Tencha guessed the age to be fourteen or fifteen. The girl was pretty, she supposed, in an Indian way. Dark-skinned, with big dark brown eyes under heavy but well-shaped brows. Her cheeks were rounded, but Tencha could see already that in time the prominent cheekbones would stand out, further emphasizing her race. The mouth was wide, the lips not very full. She was thin, and stood a bit shorter than Tencha herself, who was barely more than one and one half meters tall. Her glossy black hair was combed in a single braid. She wore it over her shoulder to the front and it ended at her waist. Loose, it would surely fall below her hips. She walked with the typical Indian carriage: small steps, head bowed, eyes lowered. It always seemed to Tencha that the *indios*, by their very demeanor, were apologizing for being alive. At the same time, this girl carried her serenity almost as a badge of honor. Really, it was to be expected of the indios, who did not give away what they were thinking or feeling.

They reached the room in which Maria Dolores was to sleep that night, and for several nights thereafter. "Descansa un rato," whispered Tencha, "and sleep if you can, because tonight we are going to the Posadas at the home of Don Higinio Casas y Vega." The girl opened her mouth as if to speak, but Tencha didn't give her a chance. "Everybody in this household goes to the Posadas. We commemorate the travels of the Virgin Mary and St. Joseph as they seek shelter in Bethlehem. It would not be proper to stay home when they had to make the journey so many years ago." With that, she turned and left the room, closing the door and leaving Maria Dolores alone.

The girl stood in the center of the room for a few minutes. She looked at the walls…they were so high! They were painted the color of clouds. She walked to one of the walls and touched it…so smooth…her gaze moved to the ceiling. It too was white, but it had no hole to let in the blessing of the sun and the sky, or to let out the smoke of the cooking fire. Indeed, you could make no cooking fire in this room, even though it was bigger than her hut.

She knelt at the picture of the Virgin of Guadalupe that was tacked up on the east wall and let her sorrow engulf her. "*Madrecita del Dios vivo*," she whispered, using the words the catechists had taught her people, "*ayúdame*. Help me to live and to do as my grandfather asked. You know what I am. Help me to be and do what I must. Give my love to those who rest in your arms." As she finished her prayer, a *zenzontle* flitted to her window. And as the mockingbird sang, Maria Dolores smiled, thanked *Cihuapili* for her answer, and fell asleep.

Tencha returned to Father Santiago's office, carrying a tray with coffee and sweet bread for his merienda. Though he was a *norteamericano*—not a *gringo*, the tourists were gringos—from Detroit, he had quickly fallen in with the rhythm of life in Mexico. His appreciation of her cooking, and his confidence in her had won her heart. She had all but adopted him, and liked to say that he was not really from Michigan, but from Michoacan, for he favored the dishes from her home state. In her eyes, he was a holy man, and because of that she could accept his softhearted approach in his dealings with the indios, though she could not totally agree with it. Still, the whole affair concerning this particular india was just too much. She could not be allowed to live in the parish house. That would be carrying his kindness too far. Tencha had to speak to him about this.

"Father Santiago," she began. "What are we going to do about la indita? I put her in Francisca's room, but Francisca will return after Christmas. Of course, I don't know why you even let Francisca go during this time; there is so much work to do." She couldn't help commenting again on his foolishness in letting Francisca go home during the holiday season. "You must know that this girl cannot take her place. I would have to train her, and for what? Anyway, when Francisca comes, there will not be any room for her." And having said her piece, she took a piece of *semita*, the anise-flavored bread that she favored, dipped a small corner of it in her coffee, and bit off a mouthful.

Father Santiago smiled and shook his head playfully. "Now, Tenchita,"—he was the only one who could get away with calling her that instead of Doña Tencha—"you would not want me to turn away someone seeking posada, especially not at this time of year, would you?" He lowered his voice, and conspiratorially added, "But don't worry yourself, I have a plan. Tonight at Don Higinio's house, I will name Maria Dolores to be the Virgin for tomorrow's Posada at the home of the Figueroas. Then I will ask Doña Elodia to take her into service. They will surely not deny this favor."

Tencha's eyes crackled. "But how are you going to name her to be the Virgin! She is too…. too…too Indian! It cannot be! Father Santiago, don't do this thing you are thinking of. You should name one of the local girls, girls from good families, who know what this means. It is not right." Tencha stood up and straightened her 5'3" frame. "You cannot do this. Padre Santiago, listen to reason, please."

The priest stood up also. At 6'2", he towered over the woman. He placed both hands on his desk and brought his face to her level. His jaw clenched and unclenched, and the little vein in his right temple pulsed dangerously. "Tencha, what would La Virgen Morena say to you right now?" he reprimanded. "Don't forget that it was for the indios that Our Lady of Guadalupe appeared to Juan Diego. Maria Dolores is going to be the Virgin tomorrow, and nothing is going to change my mind." He punctuated the last three words by pounding on the desk, and stalked out of his office. He had to admit to himself that he had romanticized the Mexicans, thinking they were such loving people. Yet in the six years he had spent at this parish, he encountered hatred against the indios many times. To have Tencha say it out so blatantly had ticked him off.

Tencha sank down in her chair and fought the tears that threatened. She had never seen Father so angry! And never before had his anger been directed at her. For a few minutes she just sat there and pondered the situation. It was true that Our Lady of Guadalupe was morena, dark-skinned, but the virgin of the Posadas was the Virgin of the Incarnation, and she was not dark. Father Santiago was just too holy a man to understand these things. La Virgen de Guadalupe was fine for the indios, but she was not the main virgin, like the Virgin of the Incarnation was. Yes, she had heard all the teachings about how it was always the same virgin, but in different apparitions, or at different times. But one could not help it if the white virgins were more beautiful, more—more appropriate. Still, he was planning to get Elodia Figueroa to take the girl in. Tencha knew that Elodia didn't care for the indios either, but if the girl had been the virgin, she would not refuse Father Santiago. Yes, she could see that he was right. It would be best for the girl to be the virgin tomorrow night. She gathered the dishes from the merienda, took them to the kitchen, and went in search of Father Santiago.

She found him in the church, kneeling before the statue of Our Lady of Guadalupe that was placed in a special niche at the entrance to the temple. She herself preferred to pray before the painting of the Immaculate Conception that was placed near the main altar. But she was not here to pray. She knelt in a pew nearby, waiting for him to finish. He turned around when he felt her presence, and went over to her. "Tencha, forgive me for yelling at you. It's just that I think it's important that you understand that the indios are children of God too, and that..."

"Father Santiago, I know what you are saying. And you are right." She turned around so that he couldn't read in her face that she still did not agree with him. "The indita must be the virgin tomorrow night. It will pave the way for her future. And Doña Elodia will be proud to have her in service."

That evening, she watched as Father Santiago worked his magic on the Figueroas and on the rest of the people who were enjoying the reception after the evening's posadas. Oh, but he did have a way with words, even if his native language was not Spanish. He had earlier introduced Maria Dolores, talking about how the girl had selflessly worked to help the villagers who had fallen to the influenza, how she had lost both parents and finally her grandfather. (He did not mention that she had also lost her husband...but of course, if the girl was not a virgin, the people would not accept her playing the Virgin, no matter what he told them about her.) It seemed as if he had been there every minute, watching the tragic events in the village unfold. By the time he finished, several of the Figueroa's friends had gathered around them to listen to the story, each mesmerized by Father Santiago's passion, each clucking on cue about the hardships the girl had endured, each ready to proclaim her a saint, if that had been the priest's wish.

Then Father's narrative turned to the Virgin Mary, how she had selflessly gone to help her cousin Isabel during the last three months of waiting for the birth of St. John the Baptist. How the Blessed Mother had given of herself, not thinking how the hard work at her cousin's house would tire her out, she who was soon to be the Mother of God. He deftly equated Maria Dolores' selflessness to that of the Virgin, and asked the group to agree with him. Every last one of them agreed wholeheartedly. It was then that he announced that for all these reasons, he had elected Maria Dolores to play the Virgin the following night, when the Posada would be held at the Figueroa's own home!

Naturally, nobody raised an objection, even though all had thought that Isabel, the Figueroa's daughter, would play the Virgin on that night. Isabel herself agreed most vehemently. She did not want to play the Virgin, preferring to play hostess to her friends instead.

Then Father delivered the coup de grace, asking Doña Elodia if she would consider taking Maria Dolores into service. Doña Elodia had no recourse but to accept the situation; she could not lose face in front of all her friends. Father had complimented her on her generosity and charity towards the poor. Only Doña Tencha noticed the wave of annoyance that flickered in Elodia's eyes before she smiled and said it was her Christian duty to help the needy.

And so Maria Dolores reenacted the journey of the Virgin Mary, carrying her worldly possessions with her and seeking posada in the Figueroa household.

3

Maria Dolores was nervous but excited. Since last December, she had been doing laundry for the Figueroa family. It was backbreaking work, for everything had to be laundered by hand, and she had to first pump the water, then heat it to near boiling before any of the clothes came near it. After it had dried on the lines set up for the wash, every article had to be ironed, even the socks that el Señor Juan Pablo and el Jóven Juanito wore. The Señora herself inspected every item; everything had to be done just so.

The first time she'd washed the clothes, Maria Dolores had been unaware that the clotheslines even existed. She had carefully spread out the clothes over the bushes, as was the custom in her village. The Señora had been beside herself with anger. "India estúpida!" She had thrown the clothes at Maria Dolores' feet. "Don't you know any better than this? Wash those clothes again, and do it right! Just wait until I tell my husband about this."

Fortunately, Pajita, the cook, took her over to the lines and patiently showed her how to hang up the clothes to dry. That evening, Don Juan

Pablo Figueroa Mancillas had a good laugh about the laundry incident. He even came out to see which bushes the girl had thrown the clothes over. Maria Dolores had been immensely relieved, especially when he told her not to worry, that he would not dream of kicking her out.

Estrella, the house servant, taught Maria Dolores how to fold and iron the clothes so that Doña Elodia would approve. Maria Dolores felt very comfortable with Estrella and her husband Vicente. She could see in them traces of the indigenous race and often spoke to them about her former life in the mountains. Though they did not speak any form of the Nahuatl, they had heard from their ancestors about groups of indios who lived in the mountains after having escaped the destruction brought on by the white men. Legend had it that they wandered from one end of the sierra to the other, always avoiding contact with the civilization down below.

Maria Dolores explained how her village had come to be settled. Her grandfather had a dream when she was about seven years old. In the dream, a woman he called the Lady told him to find the place near a river where there was a cactus growing around a pine tree. It was there that they should build their homes. It took them nearly thirteen cycles of the moon to find it, but one day as they were drinking at the river, he looked up and found the sign not three meters from the bank on the other side of the river.

So they had set up their village and began life as settlers instead of wanderers. They had some goats that had always accompanied them in their travels. And they would fish in the river and hunt, and gather fruits from the trees and plants that grew there.

Tlaltexolal consisted of twelve thatched-roof adobe huts that sat around a common work area. To the south, the mountain on which it perched continued up another thousand feet; fifty yards to the east, the stream that supplied water for the village babbled to the rocks and the trees on its way to the city at the foot of the mountain. Between the village and the stream, the natives had cleared the soil and planted corn, squash, and beans. In the common area, a few scrawny chickens pecked at the ground. The goats were kept in a corral near the fields.

In a matter of months, the priest found them there and slowly began to establish a relationship with Teoxihuitl, her grandfather and the elder of the village. The villagers would run away into the woods whenever he came, leaving Teoxihuitl to deal with him. One day, he brought a gift to Teoxihuitl. It was a picture of Our Lady of Guadalupe. The old man recognized her as the Lady of his dream. The rest had been relatively easy. First, they learned a bit of each other's language. Then Father Santiago introduced the two catechists who would do so much to change their lives.

In normal times, the women spent their days in the common area, grinding corn on their metates, weaving cloth, or making pottery, while the men tended to the fields, fished or hunted. Once a month a delegation of the men went down to the city, to the market where they sold pottery, cloth, and vegetables. They bought salt, potatoes, and other supplies that the village would need for the next month. Since their conversion five years before, on those months when all their wares had been sold, they would also buy one gold chain with a medal of Our Lady of Guadalupe. These chains went first to the elders, both male and female. God willing, little by little, the entire population would be able to wear a symbol of la Madrecita de todos.

Once a month also, in normal times, the catequistas from the city would come, to teach the villagers about the God of the Lady, and about her Son. They were good women, these catechist nuns who could read Spanish from the books and tell them the stories of the Lord in a language very similar to their own. Slowly, the villagers had learned enough Spanish to deal with the citadinos, the city-dwellers, on a more equal basis. So, as they had learned about the new religion, the villagers had also prospered. When the priest came every three to four months, they were ready to celebrate mass, to thank their God for the good things He had done, to baptize the children born to them, and to marry in the Church.

But then influenza had come to visit. The village became quiet; no songs of joy were sung; no daily work was done. The fields lay untended, and hushed prayers were murmured in the huts as the people who had not fallen ill tended the sick. Nearly three quarters of the villagers had died within a month, and Sor Consuelo and Sor Juana, the catechists, had literally moved into the village to help. But still, her village had died out, and so she had made her way into the city.

As she shared her story with the couple, Maria Dolores came to accept her new life, and to look forward to what was to come. And Estrella and Vicente came to see Maria Dolores almost as a daughter. Their own daughter had died in infancy, leaving them with three sons but with an emptiness nonetheless. Now Maria Dolores filled that emptiness, and both Estrella and Vicente sought her out whenever they had free time.

And now, after nine months of service, here she was, working inside the house! Pajita hovered over her, giving last minute serving instructions before the girl took the porcelain soup tureen into the formal dining room.

"Remember to serve a little bit of the onion soup to Doña Elodia first, so that she may taste it and give her approval. Then you serve Don Juan Pablo. But you wait until the Señora says so. Then you come back to the Señora, serve her, then you serve el Jóven Juanito, and finally la Señorita Isabel." She saw the look of dismay on Maria Dolores' face and added, "Don't worry, child! You'll do fine. Remember, Don Juan Pablo himself promoted you."

Maria Dolores took the tureen, went straight to Mrs. Figueroa and served half a ladle of soup. Elodia tasted the soup, nodded her approval, and told the girl to proceed. Maria Dolores took the soup to the other end of the table and served Don Juan Pablo, who thanked and complimented her. As she returned to the Señora, her foot slipped, and she almost dropped the tureen. Don Juan Pablo and his nineteen-year-old son rushed to her side; the son took the tureen from her hands while the father held her by the elbows to steady her. "Be careful, Maria Dolores. We wouldn't want you to hurt yourself," he said.

Elodia watched as the two men made fools of themselves. "That's right; serving soup is such a dangerous thing." She continued, "Perhaps we should let Pajita finish serving the meal."

Her husband gave her a look that brooked no argument. "Nonsense. It was nothing. The girl may finish doing her job." He resumed his seat at the head of the table and started eating his soup. After two spoonfuls, he addressed his daughter. "Tell me, Isabel, how was your day? Did you go to the party at Rosalinda's? How are the plans for her wedding coming along?"

Isabel, eager to sidetrack one of her mother's well-known shows of Spanish temper, launched into a detailed description of the afternoon party and Rosalinda's wedding plans, knowing that would break the tension that had surrounded them. She turned to her brother. "Juan Angel, guess who was there? Carolina Holguin Cano. She asked about you," she teased. She knew her brother had a crush on Carolina. She also knew that her mother had plans for Juan Angel and Carolina, and would appreciate this little conversation. She was right. Her mother had been silent, stony after her father had rebuked her. Now she leaned forward, interested in what was coming.

Juan Angel took the bait. "So what? Este…What did she say?" He looked at the three sets of raised eyebrows and turned scarlet. "I mean, why would she ask about me?" The bantering continued from there and the meal ended on a pleasant note for the family.

Maria Dolores heard only bits and pieces of the conversation as she served the family their dinners. She was still a bit shaken up, for although all seemed well, Doña Elodia had been giving her strange looks all evening. She prayed as she picked up the dishes after the family had retired to the living room. "Madrecita linda de Dios, help me to do the things right; do not let me be clumsy. I know I have much to learn, but I will try to learn it quickly, if you help me. Thank you for the kindness shown by Don Juan Pablo. And please soften the heart of Doña Elodia. I try to do the things that please her, but pleasing her is hard. Thank you, Madrecita, for your help."

She had not noticed that Doña Elodia had stepped into the dining room as she was praying. Elodia had been stopped cold by the sound of the girl's voice. She hated the singsong quality of the Indian speech. And to hear the girl praying to the Indian virgin about her…it was too much. But instead of confronting the girl right then, she silently backed away from the door and retired to her room.

Elodia Esparza de Figueroa sat at her dressing table, brushing her hair with quick, furious strokes. She paid no attention to her hair, or to the array of expensive imported perfumes and creams sitting before her. "The nerve of that girl! Praying to her Virgin to soften my heart! I'll show her a soft heart. That india will not get the best of me."

At forty, Elodia was a formidable woman. Though she had never been a great beauty, she had aged well. The oily complexion that had so troubled her when she was young now served her well, for her fair skin was smooth and unwrinkled. She had green eyes, the color of emeralds, and blonde hair that cascaded halfway down her back when she unpinned the chignon she normally wore at her neck. She had, despite two births and two miscarriages, maintained her figure.

As she had aged, Elodia's bearing had become regal and her demeanor imperial; few people dared to joke with her, fewer still to contradict her. Those who did either soon regretted it. This of course did not include her husband. He was definitely the head of their family, though he generally let her reign supreme in matters pertaining to running the household.

But ever since that india maldita came into her service, Juan Pablo had gone against her, time and again, in matters relating to the girl. She had noticed the way he looked at the girl last December. That should have been enough of a warning. But Father Santiago had been so convincing in front of all her friends. "Poor thing, she's an orphan. She's young, but she works hard and will be a wonderful addition to your staff." Hah! Elodia knew how these Indians were. Sure, they acted respectful, head always bowed and eyes lowered, but that was just their way of attracting attention.

Her mother had told her many times never to allow an india to serve in her household. She had told her how her own father, Elodia's grandfather, had succumbed to the temptations presented by an india and kept her in their very home. The woman had been a thorn in her grandmother's life, bearing two bastards for the grandfather, two bastards who eventually inherited a part of the fortune destined for Elodia's mother, Genoveva. When the father had died, Elodia's grandmother moved to Mexico City with Genoveva. But her spirit had been broken by the heartache. She had gone to an early grave, still mourning the loss of her husband's love. The indias just could not be trusted.

But this was a deeply guarded secret; she had told no one this story, not even her husband, so naturally, she had said none of these things to the priest. Besides, the idiot gringo would have said she lacked Christian charity, that you cannot judge all people by the actions of one. Stupid man.

And now it seemed to her that Juan Pablo was getting dangerously close to bedding the girl. Normally, she would not have minded if her husband found himself a mistress. Then he would be less of a nuisance to her—but Juan Pablo had always been faithful. So if he took this one to bed, it would mean he cared for her. That would never do. If the girl bore him a child, Juan Pablo would take responsibility, and her own children would be deprived of their patrimony. No, she would not allow that to happen, no matter what.

The problem was, of course, how to get rid of the girl without damaging her own reputation in the process. Elodia resumed her brushing, more slowly now. She couldn't just fire the girl, not after all the fuss Father Santiago had made about Elodia's kindness in front of all her friends. And she would never intimate that her husband, the descendant of a fine and respected Spanish family, would stoop so low as to be interested in a backward Indian.

Elodia slid the silver back of the brush across her cheek and down her neck as she mused about getting rid of Maria Dolores. Somehow, she had to find a way to make Juan Pablo fire the girl. And to make it so that no one would step in and help her. She placed the brush next to the matching comb and hand mirror on the dressing table and braided her hair as she readied for bed.

She picked up a jar of French face cream and applied it to her face in small, precise circles as she ruminated. She moved down the base of the throat and applied the cream in long, upward strokes. Eyes closed, she moved down to her chest, applying cream to the tops of her breasts and up to her shoulders. Finally, she opened her eyes, put the jar back in its place, and looked into her reflection in the gilded oval mirror on the wall.

She smiled. It would require no small measure of her acting powers, but a plan, a perfect plan, had been made.

4

Maria Dolores swept the kitchen carefully, musing on her good fortune. She had been helping Pajita for a week now, with no unpleasant incident. Even Doña Elodia had softened toward her, gracing her with a smile every now and then. This morning, Don Juan Pablo announced that he had invited Father Santiago to dinner this evening, and, because it was Friday, the cooks were to prepare a seafood dinner. Doña Elodia herself had gone to the market early this morning to purchase the ingredients, and then she and Isabel were spending the day in town, for they hated the smell of seafood as it cooked. Maria Dolores hoped she would have a chance to speak to the priest, to thank him again for all his help.

Pajita bustled into the kitchen, cheerily talking to Maria Dolores, telling her about the plans for the big meal. She had been called in to Mrs. Figueroa's room, to receive instructions for the meal. Today they would prepare paella. They would also make a light fish soup, fresh vegetable salad, and for dessert, flan. "And guess what, Maria Dolores," she beamed, "Doña Elodia has asked me to teach you how to prepare the dishes!" She hugged Maria Dolores and then clasped her hands. "I told you everything would be all right. If Doña Elodia is asking for you to learn to cook, it means that she has confidence in you, that you are accepted for real, and that you will always have a home with this family, as long as you want. Now hurry and finish with the sweeping so that we may get started."

Pajita's fond gaze followed Maria Dolores as the girl set about her duties. Her mind wandered back to when she herself had started working for the Figueroa family. Don Juan Pablo had been but a child, only eleven years old, and Pajita a twenty-seven year old widow with a nine-year-old son. The only skill she had to offer was cooking, and it was evidenced in her plump frame. Juan Pablo's parents had taken her in, and even helped with her son's education. He had studied law, and now had his own practice in Guadalajara. Many times he had asked her to come live with him and his family, but her loyalty to the Figueroas kept her in their employ. After the death of the older couple, Juan Pablo had asked her to work for him, and she had not been able to deny him, even though she did not care for Doña Elodia. But she was past sixty now, and arthritis had started an insidious assault on her body. She would like to retire soon, and spend a few years with her son and his family, before she became unable to make their favorite dishes. Perhaps, if Maria Dolores learned quickly, she would be able to leave by the time Christmas rolled around.

"What do you think, Pajita?" Maria Dolores' voice broke through her reverie.

"What?" responded Pajita. "What did you say, girl? I'm sorry, I wasn't listening."

"I was wondering if I would get a chance to talk to Father Santiago tonight." Maria Dolores tightened her grip on the broom handle. "There is so much I want to tell him. He doesn't even know that I'm working in the kitchen now. He's the one who convinced Doña Elodia to take me in, and I want to thank him properly." She took a small package from the pantry shelf. "I made this stole for him. It's for the Feast of Our Lady of Guadalupe. Look." She handed the package to Pajita.

Pajita carefully unwrapped the package and removed the stole. It was truly amazing! On the right side of the pale blue stole was the image of the Virgin, perfectly wrought in embroidery. On the left side knelt the indio Juan Diego, hat in hand. The borders were embroidered in roses of all colors. Pajita carried the stole to the door, to see it in natural light. She played her fingers lightly over the embroidery. "You made this, Maria Dolores? But when? How? I didn't know you could do this fine work!"

"It is done well, then? The catechists, Consuelo and Juana, gave us lessons. They said we could do this to our cloth, to make it pretty so that the city people would want to buy it. I thought Father Santiago would like it, because he has such a great love of the Lady." A wisp of sadness crossed her face. "My village is no more; my family is dead. But my grandfather taught me to be grateful to the Virgin and to her Son, and to show the gratitude. So I made this for Father Santiago, because he was the one that the Virgin used to help me make my way. Do you think he will accept it?"

"Accept it? He will love it and wear it proudly. I think he will even show it to other priests and tell them how an Indian girl who has no education can still express her love of God in such a beautiful way. Oh, Maria Dolores, always remember that God has given you much. You can work, and you can love, and you can sew such fine things. And now it is also time to cook; we do not want to leave the family hungry tonight!" She carefully folded the stole, rewrapped the package, and placed it on the pantry shelf. She took Maria Dolores's hand. "Come now; it is time to begin your lessons in European cooking."

5

Father James Mallory, called Padre Santiago by his parishioners, folded his lean frame into the chair as he put on his shoes. He was worried about Maria Dolores, after the surprise visit by Doña Elodia this afternoon. He found it nearly impossible to imagine the somber girl acting the coquette, but the woman had no reason to lie about such a thing.

"Padre Santiago," the woman had begun. Her green eyes had met his for a moment, then lowered in the demure way these Mexican women had. She twisted her dainty handkerchief, untwisted it, then continued, "I don't know how to say it, except to say it plainly. Maria Dolores is flirting with Vicente, the husband of Estrella, who cleans the bedrooms in our household. Estrella doesn't know it, and I think the man is innocent; but I have seen the looks Maria Dolores is giving him, and I know of these things." She had paused, moistened her lips and looked at him.

He fidgeted in his chair but said nothing, so she resumed, "In truth, I think even Maria Dolores is unaware of what she is doing. I don't believe anything has happened between them, but she is falling in love with him.

You know, she is working in the kitchen now; Juan Pablo himself promoted her, and I did not object, because she is a hard worker and very respectful, like most of the indios. But now I am worried that she will fall into…" she paused, then almost whispered the final word, "…sin."

Father Santiago felt the blood drain from his face. He had promised Don Diego that he would help the girl. But now…how could something like this be happening? He called up an image of the girl as she prayed, for she often went to the church to pray before the statue of Our Lady of Guadalupe, and could not match it to what Doña Elodia was saying. Still, the woman seemed genuinely concerned. "Doña Elodia, if Maria Dolores is doing something improper, then you have a perfect right to…"

"Oh, but Father, you don't understand. I want to help Maria Dolores. I think the girl is just lonely; she has lost her entire family, indeed, all her village. She needs to be distracted, to see other things, and maybe she will understand that she is headed in the wrong direction. No, I don't want to just let her go; that would not be the Christian thing to do; I want to help her.

"I know that she had promised to help here, in the parish house, when my husband and I go on vacation next week. I think if she does that, she will be too close to Estrella and her husband, because Vicente will be doing some maintenance work at the house. I think the temptation will be too great.

"What I would like to do is take her with us to Tampico. We had planned to go to Mazatlán, but Juan Pablo has some business in Tampico, and we will take advantage of that to take our vacation there. Now, we don't usually take any of our servants with us, but I would like to make an exception this time. I think it will be a great help to Maria Dolores. I will use the time to advise the girl, to prevent her from making a mistake."

Doña Elodia looked straight into his eyes. "But, Father Santiago, she has already given you her word, and unless you insist that she go with us, I know she will refuse. I would like for you to help me in this. Tonight, when you come to dinner, I will ask Maria Dolores to go with us to Tampico. Please back me up on this, and insist that she do so." She hesitated a moment before continuing. She seemed to be getting up her courage for something. Then she said, "And Father, I hate to ask you this, but please don't tell my husband. I'm afraid he would fire her on the spot if he suspected that she was capable of leading Vicente astray. You see, Vicente has been with us for so long."

Of course, he had agreed to help. Still, he wished there were a way he could find out for himself about Maria Dolores and Vicente. But he also knew that a man, even a priest, did not talk to the indias about such matters. So he would have to trust Doña Elodia and follow her plan. He finished dressing and went to the front door. He decided to walk the ten blocks to the Figueroas' residence. Maybe the walk would calm him down.

Doña Elodia sat at her dressing table, putting the finishing touches on her makeup. Her little talk with the gringo priest had gone very well; he had been completely convinced by her story. And now she had arranged for Vicente to be in the kitchen after dinner. When Father Santiago went back there to talk to Maria Dolores, he would find them together. She picked up a bottle of perfume and applied it carefully.

There was a soft knock at her door, and Estrella entered silently. "Señora, Don Juan Pablo has sent me to look for you. Father Santiago has arrived."

"Tell him I'll be right down. And Estrella, tell Juan Angel and Isabel that they should go downstairs now." She slipped out of her dressing gown and put on the chocolate silk dress that Estrella had laid out earlier. She opened the jewelry box and selected the gold and emerald earrings her husband had given her for their twentieth anniversary, patted her hair one more time, and walked out of the room and down the stairs.

She entered the spacious living room and found her family and the priest assembled there. "Father Santiago," she beamed, "I am so glad to see you again. I hope you enjoy the dinner we have prepared for you this evening. Juan Pablo, have you not offered Father Santiago a drink?"

"Yes, of course, my dear, but we were waiting for you. I know you want a sherry. Father, a scotch on the rocks, correct?" Juan Pablo strode to the bar as he spoke, and busied himself with the drinks. Father Santiago seemed a little nervous to him, but then you never could tell with the norteamericanos; they were always a little on edge. He returned to the group, handed the drinks all around, and settled himself on the settee.

"I was just telling Father Santiago that you and I are going to Tampico next week," his wife said. "Of course, our children will not go this time. They must attend classes still." She smiled at her son and daughter, who returned the smile. "We have a little vacation house by the sea there."

"Actually, we are mixing a little pleasure with business. I'm looking into some property there. I may be able to establish a new resort near that port." Juan Pablo sipped his cognac. "Now that the war is over, the Americans will be looking to enjoy themselves once again. And there is no reason why Tampico cannot be added to the list of vacation spots." He smiled expansively as he raised his glass in the manner of a toast.

"Juan Pablo, I've been thinking," Elodia took the opportunity to interject. "I would like to take Maria Dolores with us to Tampico. You know the poor girl has never been anywhere, and she has suffered so much." There was just a trace, a slight trace of sarcasm. It went unnoticed. "She is learning to cook now, and by the end of the month should be able at least to prepare our breakfasts. I'm sure we can hire some locals to come in during the day and prepare the major meals, but that way we won't have to find someone to live in while we're there. You know how hard it can be to trust strangers."

Juan Pablo beamed, overjoyed that perhaps his wife was finally accepting that poor Indian girl. "Mi vida, that's an excellent idea! I will tell her myself."

"There's just one little problem…I believe that she promised Father that she would help in the parish while we are gone…"

"That's not a problem at all, Doña Elodia," the priest responded on cue. "I will encourage Maria Dolores to go with you. It's an excellent opportunity for her, and I wouldn't allow her to let it slip by." He looked past Doña Elodia and saw Maria Dolores standing at the entrance to the living room. For a moment he almost didn't recognize her; the black and white maid's uniform she was wearing was a far cry from her usual peasant blouse and shirred skirt. He found his voice again and said, "Maria Dolores, we have some wonderful news for you!"

He turned to Don Juan Pablo, who told Maria Dolores about the trip. Maria Dolores was about to protest when Doña Elodia spoke up, saying it was a wonderful idea. And the priest capped it off, insisting that it would be good for her.

There was nothing left for Maria Dolores to do, except thank them for the opportunity, then inform them that the meal was ready, and that they should go into the dining room.

At the end of the meal, Vicente entered the kitchen and found Maria Dolores at the sink, washing dishes. The poor girl looked miserable, as if she wanted to cry. When he asked what the matter was, she told him that she would be going to Tampico with the Figueroas, and that she did not want to go, because she had hoped to celebrate her fifteenth birthday by going to Mass and making an offering to the Virgen de Guadalupe. Then she began to sob in earnest. He put his arms around the girl, wondering what words of wisdom he could offer.

Father Santiago walked in and found them wrapped in each other's arms. He cleared his throat, and they separated quickly, and, it seemed to him, guiltily. He looked at Vicente. "I believe Doña Elodia and Don Juan Pablo want to talk to you, Vicente."

When Vicente was gone, Father Santiago addressed the girl, "Maria Dolores, I hope you take advantage of this time in Tampico to think about your life and what you truly want to do. Doña Elodia and Don Juan Pablo are giving you an opportunity that not many in your situation get. You are a young woman, Maria Dolores, and you must take care to choose the right thing to do." That was as much as he felt he could say about the subject. He hoped it was enough, for now he was convinced about what Doña Elodia had told him.

The girl blushed and lowered her head, "Sí, Padre. I will go and serve Doña Elodia and Don Juan Pablo. I will do as you say." She looked up again, eyes brightening. "Father Santiago, may I give you something?"

"Of course, child, what is it?" He watched as she took a small package from the shelf. She handed it to him and lowered her eyes.

He unwrapped the present carefully and was astonished at the stole. "Maria Dolores, where did you get such a thing? It is just exquisite!"

"It is all right, then? I made it for you, for the Virgin. I...I used part of my wedding dress for the cloth. I hope the Virgencita will be pleased."

Father Santiago assured her it was pleasing to the Virgin and to himself. And he wondered at the same time how this girl could seek both to please the Virgin and to love a married man. He sighed. Yes, a time away from Vicente would certainly be the best thing for her.

TWO

The old man and the Lady stood on the mountain that had been his home. They walked among the ruins of the village. The plots where the maize and the vegetables had grown were gone; native plants had overtaken those that had been so carefully cultivated. Plants were growing even where the huts had stood. Soon, there would be no trace to indicate that a people had lived there.

He looked at the Lady and bowed his head. She reached out and with a gentle touch guided his face until his gaze met hers. There was a question in his eyes. She smiled softly and pointed down the mountain, toward the north. He saw the blue stone that he had cast down the mountain roll past the city, then continue northward.

It seemed to stall for a while near the eastern coast, then resumed its way toward the north. He wanted to call out, or to follow the stone, or even to pick it up, return it to the time before the journey had begun.

But he did none of these things, for they were outside his power. The Lady touched his shoulder, and together they sent a blessing after the stone.

Then the two turned and walked toward the mountain peak.

6

May 1946

Maria Dolores woke from a restless sleep. The dream was a puzzle to her, for she could remember only fragments. She knew that it was her grandfather and the Virgin, but she could not quite understand what the dream was trying to tell her. She got up early and went to the church. She had to ask Cihuapili for advice again. This was where she had come nearly eight months ago, when Doña Elodia and Don Juan Pablo threw her out of the house. She could still see the Señora's face, contorted with rage, as she yelled, "India maldita! We trusted you completely, and you thought you could get away with stealing from us. Don't try that innocent look. Here is the money we found in your room. What were you going to do? Give it to that boy who works at the butcher shop? Yes, I've seen you flirting with him." As long as she lived, Maria Dolores would not forget those words. At first, she had not understood what Doña Elodia was saying. Then it dawned on her. Doña Elodia had never accepted her at all! How could people be like this?

But worst of all was the look of disgust on Don Juan Pablo's face. And she did not deserve such treatment; she had not stolen that money. But he would not even listen to her, so she had taken her bundle of clothes and the few pesos she had with her, and had come to the church.

She had begged the Virgin for help, then gone outside, to the plaza in front of the church. As she had nowhere to go, she simply went to the first empty bench and sat down. It was there that she heard two women speaking about the hotel that was looking for workers. She followed them discreetly, hoping they would lead her to the right place. And they had. As soon as she was hired, she found a room in a vecindad, and then she went back to the church to give thanks to the Virgin.

Her life soon fell into a pattern. She would rise at 5:00, say her morning prayers, wash herself with water she had brought in the night before, make a cup of coffee and hot corn cereal, change into her work clothes and walk to work.

She started in the kitchen where she washed the big pots and pans from breakfast. Then she proceeded to clean the row of rooms that was assigned to her. At 3:00 she had a half-hour lunch break, then returned to the kitchen to wash dishes once again. She would finish her duties by 6:00 p.m. then walk home.

Her workday didn't allow her time to think, but in the evening she would sit alone in her room and pray and ponder her fate, thinking about her grandfather and what he'd said about making a better life. Here she had a pattern, a routine, yes, but something was missing. Her grandfather had taught her that everyone had a purpose in life. Here it seemed she had no purpose.

Maria Dolores met her first real friend one evening in December, when she decided to buy some pan dulce for her supper. She stopped in at the Panadería La Encantada, which had opened only three days earlier. Evita waited on her, then walked out of the bakery as Maria Dolores left. When they turned in the same direction, Evita struck up a conversation.

"You're not from around here, are you? I'm from the state of Jalisco myself. I came here to find my fortune, and fortune led me to a bakery that had just opened! Imagine that. Ah, but I'm not complaining." She ran her fingers through her thick, wavy hair, then patted her stomach. "At least I never have to go hungry!"

At this, Maria Dolores laughed. "No, señorita, you will not be hungry. You can give thanks to God for that."

"Oh! I'm sorry. I haven't even told you who I am yet. My name is Eva Hernandez Jimenes. I'm eighteen years old and I've never been in love. What about you? Wait. Let me guess. I'm very good at judging people. You have such sad eyes. I bet you have had a great tragedy in your life. Did somebody make you fall in love and then leave you?"

Maria Dolores felt her head swim with her companion's endless questions. But somehow, she felt that there was no malice whatsoever in the girl's heart. So she answered, as simply as she could. "I am Maria Dolores. My parents, my grandfather, and my husband died of a terrible plague that hit our village. I have had my troubles, yes, but I am still alive, and my grandfather asked that I go forward with my life. So now I am here."

Evita had gone from bright pink to deep scarlet as Maria Dolores spoke. "Oh, I've put my foot in it, haven't I? I'm always doing that. My mother has always said that every time I open my mouth, somebody takes a bath. I used to think she meant I threw spittle between my teeth, but really she meant that I sometimes hurt people by what I say. Oh, please forgive me! It's just that I don't think before I talk. I meant no harm."

Maria Dolores shook her head and smiled. By that time, they had walked seven blocks, and had reached the vecindad where Maria Dolores lived. She turned to say good-bye to her new friend. Evita turned too, and said, "Well, this is where I live. I like you, Maria Dolores. Maybe we can talk again sometime. I have not made too many friends yet, and I think you and I can be good friends."

Maria Dolores smiled broadly now and said, "Well, I live here too. We are neighbors! I know we can be good friends. I am glad we live near each other."

The two women forged a strong friendship, often walking home together, and going to church on those Sundays that Maria Dolores could have the day off. Sometimes they sat together in the courtyard of the vecindad, Evita crocheting and Maria Dolores embroidering. They shared their life stories bit by bit, as they created a new story together.

Evita had left her home in Guadalajara because her sinvergüenza of a father wanted to sell her into marriage to a man 40 years her senior. Her aunt on her mother's side, Catarina, had been incensed at this. "He has no shame! He hurts your mother, carrying on with another woman, a woman of the streets, who is not worthy of standing in your mother's shadow, and now he wants to sell you! I will not allow it."

Tía Catarina helped Evita escape, giving her money to get away. Evita had gone to the bus station and bought a ticket to the farthest destination she could afford. That had been Tampico. She'd soon found a job as a clerk in the bakery, and had discovered a love of the work.

Maria Dolores had gone to celebrate the twelfth of December at the church, and had lit a candle to the Virgin, thanking her for the new friend. She felt the Virgin had smiled on her that day, for some of her loneliness had abated, and she no longer dwelt so much on the past. Just as her grandfather and the catequistas had taught her, la Virgen Morena never let her down.

Now, five months later, she was back, hoping the Virgin would answer her prayer once again. Evita had told her about a wonderful place where everybody who wanted to work could find a job that paid much money. Her cousin Matilde was earning 50 cents American each day, and the family she worked for gave her room and board besides. Not only that, Matilde had Sundays off, and could stay home or go out as she pleased. It was a marvel, this place called Texas, in the United States.

At the Hotel Palmeras, Maria Dolores was earning 15 pesos a week, but she paid three pesos rent to her landlady. And after buying food and other necessities, she had but four or five pesos left, which she was saving to buy fine cloth and embroidery thread. She had hoped to make a manto de la Virgen, for the church to use in the Posadas this year. But now there was the possibility of using the 150 pesos to pay for the journey to this wonderful place. So she came to ask the Virgin for guidance. She knelt before the image of Our Lady of Guadalupe, dropped a 5-centavos coin in the collection box, and lit a small candle.

"Virgencita de Guadalupe," she began. "Cihuapili, you who live with your Son and the great Tata Dios. You, who chose to come to our people to lead us to him. You, who have with you my mother and father, my grandfather, and my husband. You, who have never left me alone, even when Doña Elodia accused me of those evil things. I come before you again to ask your favor. I ask you now and I beg you, to guide me and tell me what I should do. You see, my friend Evita—you know, the one who works at the bakery—she says we should go north, to Texas. She says there is work there, that we can make our lives new there. And I—I have nowhere left to go. I cannot go back, but here, life is…lonely. I am alone now, except for Evita. And she wants to go. I do not know what to do. Please, Virgencita, give me a sign. If you say I should go, I will. If you say I should stay, I will. I trust in you, and I will recognize the sign you give. Gracias, Madrecita." She left the church and hurried off to the hotel.

When Maria Dolores arrived at the vecindad that night, Evita rushed over to see her. "Yoli!" she panted. "Look! I got a letter from my cousin Matilde. She says there are many Americans who are looking for servants. She says if I go, she will find me a place to work. What do you say, Yolihuani? Go with me." Evita liked to use Maria Dolores's indio name once in a while. She thought it sounded pretty.

Maria Dolores looked at her friend and said, "But Evita, she says she will find you a job. But what about me? Do you think I can find work too?"

"Of course. See, it says here that many Americans want servants. And look, she gives the name of the coyote that crossed her to the other side. His name is…let me see…ah, here it is! Don Guadalupe Moreno Chavez. What do you say, Yolihuani? Go with me."

As soon as she heard the man's name, Maria Dolores was convinced. Here was the sign from the Virgin. She would go with Evita and find a job in Texas.

They made their plans quickly, and left Tampico for good on May 30, taking the cheapest seats on the least expensive bus company.

7

After a grueling 18-hour trip by bus, which included a 3-hour layover in Monterrey and stops at every little village between Monterrey and the U.S.-Mexico border, Maria Dolores and Evita arrived in Matamoros at 7:00 a.m.

Evita approached a policeman and showed him the scrap of paper on which Lupe Moreno's address was written. "Perdone, Señor Policía, can you tell me how to get to this address? We are not from here, and don't know our way around."

The policeman looked them over, then glanced down at the paper. "It says here Ejido Los Fierro. That's a little hamlet about 25 kilometers outside of Matamoros, on the way to Rio Bravo. You will have to take the bus marked "Reynosa" and ask the driver to let you off in Los Fierro. There you can ask anybody where your friend lives. It's a small place, and everybody knows everybody."

The two young women thanked him and returned to the bus station to purchase tickets to Los Fierro. The bus would leave at 1:00. They had almost five hours to kill, so they decided to walk to the plaza and get something to eat. They got directions from the same policeman who had helped them earlier, then walked the five blocks to the plaza. Though it was early, the bright sun had brought the temperature into the eighties. By the time they reached the town square, Maria Dolores and Evita could feel the sweat trickle down their backs.

Maria Dolores suggested they go into the church to cool off and rest their feet. The bells sounded for the eight o'clock daily mass. A group of girls from the Catholic school entered, carrying flowers for the Virgin. The nuns who were shepherding the girls looked at Maria Dolores and Evita with disdain and told the girls to move along to the front of the church.

One of the younger girls ran back and gave Maria Dolores and Evita each a flower, saying they could offer it to the Virgin. Maria Dolores was deeply touched by the gesture.

"What is your name, mijita?" she asked.

"Alba María Violeta Martínez de Sáenz y Peña," the girl replied, "but you can call me Violeta. That's what my nanny calls me. She's dark brown like you. And what is your name?" Just then one of the nuns came back and took the little girl by the hand.

"Alba María! How many times do we have to tell you not to talk to strangers? You do not know who or what these people are!" She half-dragged the child to the front of the church, leaving Maria Dolores and Evita standing there, flowers in their hands. They turned toward the side altar, which was dedicated to the Virgin of Guadalupe, and placed the flowers at the foot of the statue. Evita walked out of the church immediately, unable to control her shaking and her anger, but Maria Dolores stayed behind and knelt before the statue.

"Madrecita Morenita, thank you for the gift of Violetita," she whispered. "And please forgive the nun for her harsh words; she is only protecting the child. Watch over Evita and me as we continue the journey, which you have blessed. And greet my grandfather, my mother, my father and my husband, who dwell with you in the house of toteotzin." She blessed herself and went out in search of Evita.

Her friend was across the street, in the plaza. She waved to Maria Dolores, motioning for her to cross. "There is a bakery on the other side. Let's go to eat some pan dulce and drink a little coffee." After breakfast, they walked around the downtown area of Matamoros, marveling at all the goods in the stores. They went to the parian, the open market, and drank agua fresca de limón, lemonade. Finally it came time to return to the bus station and board the bus that would take them to Los Fierro.

They arrived early, and managed to sit up front, right behind the driver. Evita, who always managed to make conversation even with perfect strangers, soon found out all about the bus driver, who had originally come from Santa María de los Angeles, in Jalisco. He was married to a girl from Matamoros, and had lived in the area for fifteen years. They had five children, two boys and three girls, and managed to go to Jalisco every two years or so. His wife was a seamstress who sometimes sewed for people from Brownsville, Texas. He said he had gone to work in Texas as a bracero once, before the war, but had missed his family too much to return the following year. But yes, the money had been good. And that was where he had learned to drive the big machines, so that he was able to get this job with the bus company. It did not pay too much, but it was steady work, and it kept his family fed and clothed.

Evita told him that she and Maria Dolores were going into the United States to make their fortunes too. He had laughed a little at that, and said that some people were not meant to make fortunes. But if they were decided, then they should try to work for the gringos, because the mexicanos in Texas were excessively demanding. Oh, they were not bad people, but it seemed they felt that giving their Mexican cousins a job and a place to stay somehow entitled them to more than an honest day's work.

Maria Dolores and Evita assured him they would be careful to look for the right places to work. Soon they had reached Los Fierro, and the bus driver helped them get their belongings down from the rooftop of the bus. With a "Que Dios las bendiga," he took off, and the two young women were left to find the man who would take them into the United States.

They started walking toward what seemed the center of the village. A group of boys were playing soccer in a field, and Evita walked over to the nearest one, asking if he knew Lupe Moreno. He said sure, everyone knew Don Lupe; all they had to do was walk down to the plaza at the center of town, then go two streets to the right. Don Lupe had the depósito de cerveza y refrescos; they could not lose their way. Besides, anybody in the plaza could give them directions if they got lost.

About 10 kilometers west of his home, near the river, Guadalupe Moreno Chavez kept a small rowboat that he used to carry people across. Some months he made as much as four or even five hundred pesos. With his earnings as a coyote, taking people across the river into the United States, he had bought a small generator to provide electricity for his house. Then he had opened a depósito, and sold beer by the case or by the bottle. He had a refrigerator to keep beer cold, and did more than enough business to keep going. Most of the people in Los Fierro didn't know just how much he made in either business.

Lupe had bought a ranch in Nuevo Leon, and had planned to move there with his wife as soon as they could stock it with the best cattle. But she had died in childbirth, leaving him with a son to raise. He had not felt capable of starting anew then. He really didn't need much since his wife died, so he spent most of his days waiting for customers to come to him, or playing with his son. Most days, he sat at a square metal table in front of his house. The table, as well as the four chairs that surrounded it, was emblazoned with the red Carta Blanca logo.

He was 30 years old now, and knew he should remarry, give his son a mother, move to the ranch that was still being run by his cousin. The problem was, none of the women in the town appealed to him, and he didn't want to move to his ranch in Nuevo Leon and have some woman there marry him for his money.

He was sitting at his table, musing on this problem, when he saw the two young women approach. One was slight, apparently an Indian. The other one, though...his heart did a flip-flop as he watched her approach. She was tall for a woman, and big-boned. But her eyes, ah, her eyes were large and luminous, brown with flecks of gold in them...he could get lost in those eyes. He stood up as they neared.

"Buenas tardes, señoritas. How may I help you?" He offered his hand. The taller one took it and gave a firm shake.

"Hello. I am Eva Hernandez Jimenes, and this is Maria Dolores. We are looking for Don Lupe Moreno. The children said that we could find him here."

"A sus órdenes, Señorita. I am Lupe Moreno. How may I help you?"

Evita felt the blood rush into her cheeks. "You? Holy Mother! I expected a much older man! You are the Lupe Moreno who takes people into the United States?"

"The same. And you, Miss Hernandez...do you have someone there? A husband, perhaps? A novio?"

Evita blushed furiously. "No, I am not married...and I have no boyfriend." She wondered why he would ask such a thing. Could he be interested in her? He was so handsome.

A little boy toddled up to Lupe. "Papi? 'On'ta Chana?" Neto was still rubbing the sleep out of his eyes, from his midday nap.

Lupe bent over, picked up his son, and held him close. Then he pointed over to a pomegranate tree near the fence. "The puppy is over there. Go play with her, son."

He turned back to the two women and looked into Eva's eyes. They seemed to be filled with disappointment. "My poor son," he sighed. "Growing up without a mother is very hard for such a small child. My wife died when he was born, and he has never felt the warmth of a mother's love." He paused and looked into Evita's eyes before continuing. "Perhaps it is time I thought of finding a mother for him."

Eva felt hope welling up in her. "Yes," she said. "Perhaps it is." She blushed once again and wondered to herself how she could be so bold, and how she could think of mothering the little boy herself, when she had just now met his father.

None of this exchange was lost on Maria Dolores, who was watching the events unfold. Lupe's brown eyes simply came to life when he spoke to Evita. He wore his hair combed back, but one curl managed to escape to the front and flirt with his right eyebrow. He pushed it back as he spoke, and leaned down to hear Evita better. But Evita had never needed anyone to bend close to hear her. Maria Dolores smiled to herself. Surely there would be a wedding soon, even though neither Evita nor Lupe knew it exactly.

The three sat at the table and talked. Lupe remembered Matilde well enough. She had panicked when he was taking her across and had nearly capsized the rowboat. Then, when they had gotten to the other shore, she had been afraid to get out of the boat. Lupe had finally gotten out himself, pulled the boat onto the shore, and carried her out. Evita's eyes twinkled as she mentioned that her cousin was not the smallest of people.... how had Lupe managed to do all that by himself? He blushed furiously then slowly admitted that perhaps he was exaggerating just a bit.

The banter continued for a little while, then the conversation turned serious. They made plans to leave two nights later, when the level of the river would go down a little. Meantime, they could stay there, in his house. He had two bedrooms, and Neto would sleep with him.

At the appointed hour, they went down to the river and crossed. Maria Dolores had expected a much larger river than this, and expressed this to Lupe. He told her that the river was not wide, but it was treacherous; many people who underestimated it had not lived to regret it.

After bringing them to shore, he walked with them to the first house near the river. It belonged to his cousin Juana and her husband Samuel. He introduced the young women to the couple, who said they could stay the night, and Samuel would take them into a town called Harlingen in the morning. They invited Lupe to stay also, but he had to return, because Neto was waiting up for him. Before he left, though, he took Evita aside to speak in private. When she came back in, she told Maria Dolores that Lupe wanted to see her again. He would come see her here, at his cousin's house, in one week.

8

August had been hot, hot beyond belief. Now it was September, and there was no cooling in sight. Maria Dolores leaned on the mop as she mused about her homeland. There, it would be cool already, the mornings crisp and inviting. But her grandfather had told her to go forward and not look back, so she thought instead of her friend Evita. As she had predicted, Evita had married Lupe Moreno at the end of July, after a two-month courtship. By now they were settled in their ranch back in Nuevo Leon. And Matilde had gone back with them. That was a surprise. They had all thought Matilde was happy in the United States. Yet given the chance, she had chosen to return to Mexico. Maria Dolores hoped all would go well for her, as it had for Evita. They had invited Maria Dolores to join them, but she felt that her place was here; after all, the Virgen de Guadalupe herself had blessed her journey here.

She swished the mop in the bucket and continued her housework. The couple she worked for asked only that she keep the house clean, cook their meals, and occasionally look after the baby. Maria Dolores looked forward to those times when she could care for the Harding's six-month-old baby. In her village, she had often looked after the babies and children, when the women were working in the field or making the pottery and baskets they sold in the city. Babies were considered a special blessing from God; they signified a connection to heaven and to the Mother of all creation.

Maria Dolores whispered a little prayer as she worked. "Little Virgin of Guadalupe, even though these people do not believe in you, I ask you to help them. They are having problems right now. You know that many nights he arrives late, and she locks the door to their room. The child too is restless and unhappy. I beg you, teach them, Madrecita, so they may make a happy home for the child."

She continued to pray as she cleaned house. By the time she finished, the clock in the kitchen showed 11:00 A.M. Mrs. Harding would soon be home from the doctor's office, so Maria Dolores set about preparing la Señora's favorite lunch, an avocado and banana sandwich on white bread, slathered with mayonnaise. Apparently, that was one of the foods she had craved during her pregnancy, and she had somehow converted that craving into a favorite meal. Maria Dolores had tasted it once, at Mrs. Harding's urging, but it had not been to her liking.

Mrs. Harding came in with a smile, carrying her son. "Hi, Maria Dolores. Ben Jr. is in perfect health. Doctor Endicott says he's all over his summer cold, and that I've been doing a fine job with him." She put the baby into his crib, then walked into the kitchen. "And I saw Ben at the base. He's got a two-day leave! We're going to go for a honeymoon at the beach. You know, we never had a chance to have one before." Her eyes were bright, brighter than they had been in weeks. "We'll leave tonight and return tomorrow night. Oh, I'll be able to leave the baby with you, won't I? That'll be just perfect! Maria Dolores, this is just the chance Ben and I need to get back on track. It was so hard during the pregnancy and with the baby being sick for a while. But now, we can start over!"

She clasped Maria Dolores at the waist, picked her up and swung her around and around. "I'm so happy! I just know everything's going to be fine now." She put the housekeeper down and sat at the table to eat her sandwich.

Maria Dolores held on to the stove for a few seconds after Karen put her down. Everything was spinning around. She didn't understand everything the woman had said, but she did know happiness when she saw it. It was good to see her this way; Karen had not laughed in two months! Whatever it was, Maria Dolores would figure it out soon enough. She sighed as she set about cleaning up the lunch dishes. She heard a knock at the door, and went to the living room. Mrs. Harding was already there, opening the screen door to a man wearing a uniform.

"Telegram for Mrs. Karen Harding."

"I'm Mrs. Harding. Who's it from?"

"I don't know, ma'am. But it's from Missouri. Would you sign here, please?"

Maria Dolores watched as Karen signed, then opened the telegram. The Señora's face turned pale as she read, then she swooned. Maria Dolores rushed to her side and helped her to the sofa.

"Qué le pasa, Mrs. Harding? What say papel?"

"It's my father. He's had a heart attack. I—I must go home to see him!"

Karen started packing, found she couldn't concentrate, and sat on the bed to cry. Maria Dolores picked up the baby, who started to cry when his mother did, and handed him to Karen. Then she opened the suitcase and began to pack for la Señora. She didn't understand exactly what had happened, but she knew that it was bad, and that Karen was going away. She packed underwear first, then started picking out skirts and blouses, checking with Karen before carefully folding them and placing them in the suitcase.

By the time Ben came home that evening, Karen was all packed and ready to go. She had even made arrangements for a military transport to take her. Somehow, she had known her husband would have been of no help in that department. As she explained the situation, Ben's face became more and more sullen. "He disowned you for marrying me! And now you're supposed to go running to him? Well, you can do what you want, but I sure as heck will not go with you. You understand, Karen? And I don't want you to go either. I won't stop you, but I don't want you to go!"

"Ben, don't you see this might be the only chance I ever have to make peace with my father? I've got to go, or I'll regret it for the rest of my life. I—I can understand your not wanting to go. That's all right."

"What about little Ben? Are you taking the baby with you?"

"No, Ben. I don't think I'll be able to take care of him up there. I'll leave the baby with you. Maria Dolores will take care of him. She's very good with him. And Laurie Jenkins will look in on them every day."

Her answer mollified him, for he had sworn the old man would never meet his grandchild, not until he apologized for all the things he'd said when Ben had gone to ask for Karen's hand. The man had suspected, then verified that Karen was already pregnant, and had kicked them both out immediately, saying he wouldn't give a proper wedding to a slut.

That had been ten months ago. Now Karen felt she had to go back and see the old man before he died. Well, all right. Ben didn't like it, but he'd be o.k. So he took Karen to the airfield at 10:30 that night, and watched her board the transport that would take her to Missouri. Neither one knew how long she would be gone.

9

Instead of going straight home, Ben decided to go into the NCO club for a drink or two. Maria Dolores was taking care of the baby, and Karen was gone. He figured he could just pretend he was a bachelor for a while.

A couple of his friends were already there. "Hey, Ben! Good to see you buddy! I hear your old lady's flown home. Gives you a chance to have some fun. Hey, let me buy you a drink."

Ben joined his friends and ordered a beer. "No, man, that ain't the way to do it." Ben's friend motioned to the bartender. "A real man'll have a tequila with a beer chaser." He turned to the bartender, "Ain't that right? Here, get my friend a shot of tequila," He slapped Ben on the back. "Oh, yeah, and don't forget salt and a lime."

Each of the men paid for three rounds. As Ben got up to leave, his friend said, "Ben, old buddy, you can't leave now. The night's still young. Hey, ain't you got a two-day pass? You don't have to get up early in the morning. I know a place where they got some women'll dance with you. Tits out to here and nice round asses you can grab on to." He motioned with his hands as he spoke. "Shit, a man's gotta have his fun! Come on."

They took a cab to the Mexican side of town, to a place called Cantina El Rey. It was across the street from a Mexican-style square, on the west side of town. There was a shoe-repair shop in the middle of the block on the north side and a Mexican movie house near the corner on the south side. A few patrons were leaving that establishment. Ben watched as they rounded the corner away from the square.

He hitched up his pants and followed his friends into the cantina. The jukebox was blaring out some loud Mexican song about soldiers or something, and some four or five couples were dancing wildly in the semidarkness.

The three men took a table in the corner, where they could watch the goings-on. As soon as they'd settled in, three women approached them. The one dressed in red spoke to Ben, "Hey, Johnny, you wanna dance?" The music had changed to something slow and seductive. The woman took hold of his hands and brought him up to her. Her hips started swaying. "Come on, Johnny, this is a nice dance. You gonna like it."

His friends egged him on. "Whoo, Ben, you're in luck tonight, boy! Go on. She's hot to trot!" They turned to the other two women. "Sit right down, ladies. Let's have a drink and watch our friends here go for it." They ordered a round of drinks as the women snuggled close.

Ben found himself swaying to the music. The woman smelled like gardenias. Her scent assaulted his senses as he held her close, closer even than Karen had ever let him. She started whispering in his ear. "You are handsome, Johnny. I like the blue eyes. You like María? Yes?" She put both arms around his neck.

She was about 5'2 and wore her dress tight and cut low, revealing voluptuous curves. Three-inch heels brought her to the perfect height for him. Her soft black hair hung in loose waves that reached below her waist. He started touching it, smoothing it back, until he reached her buttocks. He held his hands there as they continued the dance. "I like María, yes," he said. He squeezed her gently, and María took his hands and placed them at her waist.

"Not so fast, Johnny," she murmured. "Is just a dance. You buy María a drink, many drinks. And we dance more. María likes to dance."

"No, honey, no drinks. I just wanna dance." He slid his hands back down. "And some of this. Don't you have a room in the back where we can be alone?" He nuzzled her neck, pressing her tight against his body, insinuating one leg between her legs. "I know you want some of this. You Mexican babies know how to appreciate a man."

María tried to push him off. "Pendejo, pos qué te crees?" she hissed.

Ben grabbed her tighter and kissed her roughly as she struggled against him. When she realized he would not be pushed off, she scratched his cheek and let out a yell when he backed his face away. The bartender came out from behind the bar, asking the woman what was the matter. She started rattling off to him in Spanish, and a couple of other men stood up and approached.

Ben's friends had been laughing as they watched the scene develop. Now they came up and paid the bartender, with a little extra "for the trouble." They took Ben outside and got into a cab. "I guess that's the last time we go into that cantina. Ben, you don't know when to stop, do you?" They were laughing and shouting. "I guess it's time we take this boy home. Whoo, boy, but don't he like to party!"

They had the driver drop Ben off at home, and led him up to the doorstep. "It's up to you to get yourself in, buddy."

He fumbled with the key, finally opened the door and made it inside. He got as far as the living room sofa and plopped down, with his head leaning back against the bolster. He slipped off his pants and his shirt and threw them on the floor. Within minutes he was snoring.

Maria Dolores stepped out of her bedroom. She had heard the commotion as the men left Ben at the door. She was frightened, but determined to find out what had happened. When she saw Ben on the sofa, she was relieved, and went into the other bedroom to get him a blanket. She had managed to slide him down into a lying position and was covering him with it when he opened his eyes.

Maria Dolores was wearing a thin red cotton nightgown that Karen had given her. It was sleeveless, with a scoop neck.

"Karen? Oh, Karen, honey, you're here!" Ben put his hands on her waist. "I'm so glad you didn't leave, honey. I knew you loved me more than your old man." He sat up, bringing the girl face up onto his lap. His left hand was behind her neck, holding her up to him as he kissed her. His right traveled down her body until it reached her knees, and swept her up on the sofa. He pushed the nightgown up as his hand came back up her body. "Man, I'm so hot, honey." He held her tighter and started caressing her exposed breasts roughly. Then he grabbed her by the neck and brought her mouth to his lips.

Maria Dolores was too startled to react at first, then realized what was happening. "No, Señor! Yo no soy la Señora! Please, Señor, let me go." She struggled against him, but when he sat up she was caught in his grasp. "No, no, Señor! Soy María Y…" Her cries were muffled with his kisses.

"María? It's you, María? Oh yeah. Karen's gone home to her daddy. But you're here, María. Ooh, baby, I knew you'd come around. I'm going to give it to you like you've never had it before. You'll be begging me for more, and I won't even have to pay for it," he crooned. "Let's just get rid of this little problem." He slipped the nightgown over her head and mauled her breasts. Her arms were caught in the gown, and he held them behind her with his right hand. Maria Dolores started sobbing. "Yes, María, I'm gonna love you." His left hand slipped down inside her panties, and he began rubbing, slowly at first, then more insistently. "You like that, baby? I got something you're gonna like even more." He laid her on the sofa as he stood to take off his shorts.

Maria Dolores seized the opportunity and got up quickly. She tried to run to her bedroom, but he caught up to her at the door, grabbing her by the waist and turning her to face him. "María, honey, don't play hard to get. I know you want it. I just want to love you." He took her hand and brought it down to his penis. "Look at what you do to me. You want that, don't you?"

He brought her down to the floor and pinned her arms with one hand. With the other, he ripped the panties off her, then began mauling her breasts once again. He opened her legs with his knees and thrust, penetrating her hard. It hurt so much.

She was still saying, "No, no, no.," her voice reduced to a hoarse whisper, as Ben climaxed. He slumped over her, then rolled over and fell asleep.

Maria Dolores turned on her side, curled into a ball, and cried.

After a while—it could have been minutes or hours—she got up and went into the bathroom. She locked the door carefully and ran hot water into the tub. She stepped in and sat down, bringing her knees up. She put her forehead on her knees, put her arms around her legs, and began to cry once more. Her hair fell around her, covering her face, her back, her legs, becoming a blue-black shroud for her shame, for her pain.

The water turned cold around her. Finally she took the bar of soap and began washing herself, gently at first then harder and harder, scrubbing until she could scrub no more. She stepped out of the tub only to realize that she'd brought no clothes in with her. She grabbed a sheet from the linen closet and wound it around herself. She put her ear to the door and, hearing nothing, opened the door a crack. Nothing. She looked out and crept down the hall. Ben was not in the living room. She ran to her room, locking the door behind her. Tears began streaming down her face again as she dressed.

She sat on the bed and tried to pray. "Virgencita de Guadalupe, ¿'ora qué voy a hacer?" She had never felt so alone, not even when her grandfather had died. Evita and Matilde were gone; no one here knew her.

Where could she go? She could not stay here, not even to wait for la Señora to return. And she could never face el Señor again.

So she packed her clothes and other belongings into a sack and waited for the morning. Mrs. Harding had been generous, paying her $15 a month. Before she left, she had given Maria Dolores another $20, for taking care of the baby in her absence. She added these to the $45 she had saved up, and put the money into a little bag, which she tied to her waist, under her dress. At first light she slipped out and walked away from the house, away from the neighborhood, the sun at her back. She walked towards the center of town, though she did not know it.

As she walked, she resolved to put the matter behind her. She would mention it to no one; she would survive this as she had survived the plague in her village, as she had survived Doña Elodia's accusations, as she had survived in Tampico, as she had survived the journey to this land. She would look forward always, never back.

She walked past the high school and into another neighborhood. Until now, she had walked unaware of her surroundings. Now she looked around; she had never been past the high school before. As she walked down the sidewalk, she noticed a little girl, about three years old, playing in the middle of the street. There was a car coming down the street. Maria Dolores ran to the little girl, picked her up, and carried her to the sidewalk. The mother ran out and took the child in her arms. She invited Maria Dolores in for a cup of coffee, and within half an hour hired her as a maid.

10

Maria Dolores had nearly put the rape out of her mind completely when she started to experience morning sickness. The woman she was working for gave her ten dollars and told her she would have to leave, that she could not have an unmarried pregnant woman working for her. It just wouldn't be right.

So Maria Dolores walked toward the west once again, past the downtown area, finally crossing the railroad tracks. Here things looked and felt different. The people in the street were speaking Spanish; she could ask questions and they were answered. She soon found a room in a boarding house, at 25 cents a day, payable a week at a time.

The owner was a dour-faced, sharp-tongued widow who collected the week's rent on Sunday evenings and meddled in everyone's affairs. Boarders usually lasted no more than two or three weeks. Doña Macaria, it was whispered in the halls, had driven her poor husband to the grave. Others said she had the evil eye and could kill, or at least cause great illness, with one look. So, they quickly sought other accommodations, and some-times left in the middle of the week, with two or three days' board paid up and unused.

When Maria Dolores approached her to rent a room, the woman had asked her point blank how far along she was. Then she said Maria Dolores could stay three months, no longer. The woman did not want to end up with a child on the premises. She herself had not had any children (thanks to God), and she would not stand for such in her home.

Maria Dolores quickly fell into a pattern there, taking a walk after breakfast, going to the plaza and walking past the movie house, then going to the Catholic church that was near there. She would return at about ten and work on a layette for her child. After lunch, she would take a nap, sleeping away the long afternoons. In the evenings, she would wash and iron clothes for some of the male boarders, charging five cents for pants, three for shirts. When the weather was too miserable, she would stay in all day. Those days were especially hard on her, because Doña Macaria felt it was her right to come in and harp on her plans for the future. The problem was, she had no plans for the future. She had been told that she was going to have a baby, but it was not real to her. The morning sickness had passed, and la comadre did not come visit every month, as she had since Yolihuani was 13 years old. But she did not feel as though she were carrying new life.

Her one bright spot came in December, for she was able to go to the church and celebrate first the feast day of Guadalupe and then the Christmas holy day. Even Doña Macaria had acted out of character on those days; she had accompanied Maria Dolores to the church and taken part in the celebrations. She made tamales and pan de polvo, and invited all her boarders to partake. The boarders were grateful to her, and if the tamales had less meat than the ones they had back home, well, what could they expect from Doña Macaria, after all? The pan de polvo was definitely a hit, with just the right touches of sugar and cinnamon.

But as soon as the holidays were over, Doña Macaria remembered herself. She told Maria Dolores that she would have to leave at the end of January. Maria Dolores tried to find another place, but all rooms in the vicinity were either taken or unavailable to a woman in her condition. One day late in the month, Maria Dolores found herself in the plaza. She was crying silently, desperately. A woman approached her and asked if she could help. Maria Dolores shook her head no, and said, "Not unless you have a job and a room for me."

The woman looked at her closely. "Soy cantinera. I work in that bar over there." She pointed to the Cantina El Rey. "I serve drinks and dance with the customers, to make them drink more. I make them think that I will lie with them, but I don't." She seemed to be waiting for Maria Dolores to say something.

"I—I have never been in a cantina. I'm just an Indian from the mountains in Mexico. I was working as a servant but…but…"

"But you turned up pregnant and they let you go, right? And the cabrón who got you in this mess? Did he just disappear…or was he your patrón?" Maria Dolores started crying again. "Well, no matter. If you want, you can come live with me. I will talk to Guillermo—he's the owner of the bar—to let you clean the cantina in the mornings, before the customers come."

And so Maria Dolores came to live with María Rosales. Guillermo gave her the job María had spoken about and even offered her a position as a cantinera, but later…. when her problem was resolved. The two women never talked much; María's job kept her out till two a.m., and she slept most of the day. While she slept, Maria Dolores went to the bar to sweep and mop, then walked around the plaza and went to church to pray. She would return to the house where they lived around three in afternoon, prepare a meal for María, and help her dress for work. She marveled at the clothes that María wore to work: always skin-tight, with a low bodice that showed most of her ample breasts.

Once Maria caught Maria Dolores looking at her. She said, "I told you,

Maria Dolores. I let the men think I will lie with them, but I do not. I am a barmaid, but I am not a puta. I work in the bar because I have to. I do not have any skills. And I must eat. My parents are dead. My brother, well, I do not know where he is. I am alone."

Maria Dolores told her that she knew of her goodness. "Other people may judge you, Maria, and think you are bad, but I know what you do, and who you are. I pray every day for you to the Virgen Morena, that you may find your way in this world, that you may not suffer any more. I know that she is listening, and that my prayers will be answered."

Life again took on a pattern that Maria Dolores could live with. She felt content, if not exactly happy. The baby would kick much during the day, but at night would allow her to rest. She began to consider this baby as a special gift from the Virgin, a continuation of her family. It gave her life a purpose. When she was alone, as she cleaned the bar, she would speak to her baby about her ancestors, the ancient way of life, and about Cihuapili, who was so important to her, and of the Lady's baby, Jesus. She would speak also to her grandfather, asking for the guidance to raise her child as it should be raised.

One evening, almost two months to the day since she'd invited Maria Dolores to live with her, María came in early. She was not alone. The man who was with her, she explained, was her brother. He had found out what she was doing, and had come to get her. He and his wife lived in Corpus Christi, and María could get a new start there. She told Maria Dolores that the rent was paid for the next three months (thanks to her brother), and that Maria Dolores could stay there. She gave her directions to the house of Doña Chucha la partera, telling her that the old midwife would help her when the time came to have her baby.

The Virgen had answered her prayers, but now Maria Dolores was left alone with her baby on the way.

THREE

The Lady and the old man stood on the mountain, on the faraway mountain where her village had stood, but somehow they were also close by, almost hovering over her. They were bathed in light, but a heavy darkness surrounded her. She opened her mouth to speak to them, but no sound came out. She tried to lift her arms to reach out to them, but her arms would not obey. She felt heavy, very heavy, and could not move. In her heart there was mourning tinged with joy.

She watched as the old man picked up the blue stone and caressed it tenderly. The Lady touched it too, then motioned for him to let it down again. The stone continued its roll, then hit a rock and broke into three pieces. The Lady took the old man by the hand and they turned to go up the mountain. Both nodded in her direction, as if aware that she was watching, then walked up the mountain.

She wanted to go with them, to join them, to rest forever on the mountain that had been her childhood home. The dream faded to total darkness, but she felt that it was not over. Perhaps it would never be over.

11

April 1947

Maria Dolores resumed her pattern, but it soon became difficult to do the cleaning in the cantina. She was not yet eight months pregnant, but had grown so much that it seemed she was ready to give birth at any time. Guillermo told her to take time off until the baby arrived; she was no longer cleaning to his satisfaction.

Maria Dolores did not know what to do. She had been told that the partera charged $25.00 for the birthing, and she had that amount saved up. But though the rent was paid, she had relied on her earnings at the bar to buy food and other necessities. The neighbors around the house where she lived did not speak to her; they considered all barmaids to be beneath their dignity. Indeed, it was whispered among them that she was pregnant because she had been prostituting herself.

She stayed indoors for the next week, eating only corn tortillas with coffee. On Saturday, she felt the first twinges of pain in her abdomen.

First she thought they were stomach pains, but as they continued she realized what was happening.

At first light on Sunday, she walked to Doña Chucha's. The midwife looked her over and said she would be having her baby very soon. She insisted that Maria Dolores stay there. Maria Dolores gave her the $25.00, and the partera set about getting everything ready for the birthing.

Doña Chucha looked at the girl as she went through the throes of childbirth. The indita would not yell, even though she seemed to be in a great deal of pain. "Grita, muchacha, que al cabo yo estoy casi sorda. Nada me va a molestar," she said. "I don't care if you scream; that's the way we come into this world, amid screams and crying ourselves. The trick is not to leave it that way." Finally, Maria Dolores gave a hard push, and the baby came out. It was not breathing. Doña Chucha picked it up by its feet and prepared to spank it when she looked over at the girl and saw that she had passed out.

Quickly the old woman put the baby down, and rushed over to the young woman. "Muchacha! Ya pasó!" She picked up Maria Dolores' hand and it felt cold, clammy to the touch. Then she put her fingers on the pulse point on the neck, and could find no pulse. In a panic, she called out to her grandson. "Clemente! Ven acá!" When he stood at the door, she told him to help her get the girl out of her house. "If they find her here, they'll send me to jail. Let's put her out on the corner. Then you go call the police from the store. Tell them that there is a woman passed out there. They will pick her up."

They did as planned, and when she returned to her house, Doña Chucha realized she had forgotten the baby. She went over to the bed and saw that it was alive. As she prepared to take it out, she heard the wail of the police car, and stood still. She dared not take it out now. She would take care of it later.

12

Marina stood at the window of her hospital room, looking at nothing in particular. The window was open, and a gentle breeze billowed the curtains inward. She toyed with her wristwatch absent-mindedly. She'd just checked the time for the tenth time since awaking. It was seven in the morning, and it promised to be a hot day. Paul would come for her at ten, after his shift, after finishing his paperwork. She was going home after her third miscarriage in as many years. Yesterday Dr. Bedri told her that she'd never be able to bring a baby to term, never hold her own child, never be a mother.

"I know it's hard, Marina," he'd said. "But maybe later you and Paul can consider adoption. There are many children who are looking for a good home. I know from watching you work with the babies here that you'd make a wonderful mother. But God in His wisdom knows what He has planned for you."

Marina dried the tears that were welling up in her eyes. Paul had seemed oddly relieved when he'd found out about the miscarriage. Oh, he was tender with her, but something in his eyes belied the truth. Perhaps it was for the best. She and Paul had been married three years ago, in New Jersey, after a whirlwind romance. She had been a USO volunteer, and he an Air Force sergeant who had somehow never been sent overseas. He was so handsome in his uniform, and so filled with patriotic fire…and so distressed that he was being sent to Texas instead of Europe or the Pacific. She sat with him and told stories and danced with him and listened to him that day and almost every day for the next three weeks. He knew she was a war widow, that her husband had been killed near Palermo, Italy in 1943. But he didn't mind. He knew that she had been a true and faithful wife to David. And he knew that she would be a true and faithful wife to him as well. So five days before he was scheduled to leave, he asked her to marry him, she said yes, and Father Kelly cleared all the paperwork necessary for a quick wedding. She really didn't even begin to know him until they were settled in Harlingen.

As a trainer of new recruits, Paul was on call 24 hours a day, it seemed, and she threw herself into volunteer work at Immaculate Heart of Mary Church and at Valley Baptist Hospital. Her mother had told her, "Marina, get to know the priests and the doctors. You never know when you need either!" That advice had served her well.

It was through her work with the Church that she had found the house they were living in now, over on H Street. Paul hadn't really cared for the neighborhood, but she had been so excited about it. She didn't like the base housing, and she'd found out that she was pregnant with their first child, so Paul had acceded to her wishes. He never mingled with the neighbors, but he didn't keep her from socializing when he wasn't home. So she had made friends with Margarita Torres and with Dorita Lerma. Those two had been her pillars when she lost the first two babies.

"I guess I'll just have to help you mother your four children, Maggie," Marina thought.

She heard footsteps outside her door and realized that the hospital morning routine had begun. She knew that it was just about feeding time, so she walked out and turned left, toward the nursery, determined to make herself useful while she waited for Paul. She found the nurses huddled over one of the cribs. They were obviously talking about the baby girl and her mother. Marina caught just a bit of the conversation as she approached. "…. deported. Have you seen her? She's dark, really dark…how could she have…."

Marina stepped up to the group. "Oh, what a beautiful little girl! Does she have a name yet?" Marina asked. "Hi, Precious. Oh, look at you. You're just perfect, aren't you?" Marina turned to the nurses again. "May I hold her?"

The nurses were nonplussed. "Mrs. Henderson, you just…"

"I had a miscarriage. I lost my baby." She looked into their eyes. "Please let me hold her." The nurses moved aside to let her pick up the baby. "What's her name?"

Mrs. Lyons, the nurse in charge, said, "Violet. The mother calls her Violeta."

Marina thought the name was fitting. The baby had a shock of black hair and large dark blue eyes that would probably turn brown in time. Her skin was so fair she looked like a porcelain doll, with just a hint of rose in her cheeks. Marina stroked the baby's right cheek, and the baby instinctively turned toward the finger, making tiny suckling noises. "Are you hungry, Violet? Are you hungry, Baby Vi? Let's take you to your mommy. Yes, I'll take you to your mommy right now." She turned to Mrs. Lyons. "May I take her to her mother?"

Mrs. Lyons shook her head. "Can't right now," she whispered. "Immigration is in there with her. She's Mexican, you see. Hasn't got any papers. And no money. And probably no job, from the looks of it. They're going to deport her. Today."

Marina started trembling. "But what about the baby? I mean, the baby's been born here. What'll happen to the baby?"

The nurse shrugged. "I don't know. Sometimes they take them across with them. Sometimes they leave them behind and they become wards of the State. Either way it's tough on the babies. Unless somebody adopts them."

"Unless somebody adopts them...oh, Mrs. Lyons. I must talk to the mother. Let me talk to the mother. Please, let me talk to her!"

Mrs. Lyons considered for a moment, then the INS officers stepped out of the room. They came to the nurse's desk and said they would be picking up the girl in about an hour. They would appreciate anything the nurses could do to make the pickup smooth. As they left, Mrs. Lyons told Marina to go ahead and talk to the girl.

Marina stepped into the room and looked at the figure on the bed. "She's so young! This girl couldn't be more than sixteen or seventeen," thought Marina as she approached the bed. The girl was obviously frightened. "Yo Marina," she began. "Y tu?"

"Maria Dolores," she replied, and then started to ask questions in rapid-fire Spanish until Marina held up her hands.

"No tanto," she said, then explained that she could not understand that much. In halting Spanish, Marina explained to Maria Dolores that she wanted to adopt Violet. The girl shook her head violently, but Marina remained calm. She took the girl's hand and told her story, of the three babies she had lost, of how much she wanted a child, of how she had fallen in love with Violet. Then she told Maria Dolores that the girl could come live with her, and help raise the child. She couldn't stop the deportation, but she would give her money to come back. At this last argument, the girl became very still. Her dark eyes searched Marina's face for any sign of deception. Marina said, "Te dejo sola, para pensar. Vengo otra vez en thirty...treinta minutos." She walked out of the room, closing the door behind her, and went to the hospital chapel to pray.

Maria Dolores watched the woman leave her room. She tried to think through her situation. The last twenty-four hours had been difficult. She had gone to Doña Chucha's to have her baby, and in the throes of labor had passed out. When she awoke, she was at the hospital, and her baby girl was born. The doctor had told her she was very lucky to be alive. Then la migra was there, and told her she was going back to Mexico. Back to Mexico! There was no one there for her now. What would she do, and what would happen to her baby? And now this Señora had come and offered to adopt Violeta.

Confused and frightened, she begged the Virgin for help. "Virgencita de Guadalupe, ayúdame," she wept. "You are a mother, and you know what I feel. ¿Qué debo hacer?" She grabbed the medallion around her neck. "Madrecita, give me a sign. No puedo pensar. I don't know what to do for my baby. Ayúdame, Virgencita." She buried her face in her hands and sobbed uncontrollably.

She felt arms go around her, and a soft voice made soothing sounds. She allowed herself to be held until the sobbing subsided naturally, then she raised her head to see the woman who was holding her. Her eyes locked on the medallion Marina was wearing. It was the Virgin of Guadalupe! "Gracias, Madrecita. Tu me has contestado." Fresh tears sprang to her eyes, but she smiled as she said, "Sí, Señora, Usted será la madre de mi hija. You will be the mother of my daughter." Marina clasped her to her breast and they cried together. From now on, their lives would be inextricably linked.

There was a soft knock at the door, and Mrs. Lyons entered. The immigration officers had arrived to take Maria Dolores. Marina asked that they be allowed time for Maria Dolores to dress, and informed Mrs. Lyons that she would be adopting the baby. The nurse looked at the two and nodded. "I'll let the officer know." She left them alone.

Marina took out an envelope and gave it to Maria Dolores. The envelope contained money and a piece of paper with Marina's address. "Mi casa, su casa. I will esperarte." She helped Maria Dolores into a dress and walked with her to the door. "Adios, Maria Dolores. Gracias." She watched until the girl entered the elevator with the officer.

"Oh, Lord. Paul!" she thought. "He can't know she's Mexican!" One of the things she'd discovered about her husband was his prejudice against all people of color. He tolerated their neighbors only because he didn't have to mingle with them. She never discussed it with him; in her family, unpleasant things were never discussed. One time, when she was about eleven, she asked her mother why she didn't ever ask Father about staying out too late. Her mother had replied, "If you do not rock the boat, Marina, it will not sink." Now, as a married woman herself, she understood what her mother had meant, and she lived by it too.

Marina knew that he wouldn't accept Violet if he suspected that her ancestry was Mexican. Well, he just wouldn't find out.

She walked to the nursery and found Mrs. Lyons with Violet. She took the baby in her arms and held her close. Then she saw Paul coming towards them. "Mrs. Lyons," she whispered urgently. "Please go along with me on what I say." She turned to her husband. "Paul, Darling.... just look at this precious baby. The mother is a young girl, unmarried... She said she couldn't keep the baby, that—that her parents couldn't find out." She handed Violet to Paul. "Look at her. She's perfect. Oh, Paul, couldn't we adopt her? I mean, I can't have any children now, and this little girl is like a gift from heaven. The mother left this morning. She told me I could have the baby."

Paul looked at the baby in his arms, then at his wife. Marina's face was glowing, literally glowing. Two days ago he had thought she would never smile again. This baby was bringing her back. He glanced down, and was caught by two large blue eyes that seemed to be studying him. She was a pretty little thing. Maybe, just maybe he could be a better daddy than his own father had been. He touched her chin with his finger, and the baby gurgled happily. "Well, hello, Little Girl," he murmured. "You want to be my little girl?" To Marina, "I guess I can't say no to the two prettiest girls in the world!"

Marina's volunteer work in the hospital proved to be invaluable, for the administration helped her beyond her wildest expectations. Violet's birth registration named Marina and Paul as the natural parents. Marina discreetly paid for Maria Dolores's hospital bill, using money she had inherited from her mother. It seemed both sides had come out ahead.

13

Maria Dolores got into the green truck the immigration officers led her to. There were five other people in it, all illegals who had been rounded up in the fields around Harlingen. There was a metal cage barrier between the illegals and the two officers in front. She closed her eyes and whispered a quiet prayer to the Virgin. The others started talking among themselves, musing about where they would be sent this time. Maria Dolores opened her eyes and asked timidly if they weren't going to Matamoros. They laughed and said no, that would make it too easy for them. One volunteered that he had been taken as far as Mexicali one time. Another said he had visited Piedras Negras and Nogales, thanks to la migra. With each bit of information, Maria Dolores felt her hopes dwindle more and more. She had thought to return within two days. Now she didn't know how long it would take. The twenty dollars that Marina had given her would bring her back from Matamoros. But from these other places? Maria Dolores did not even know where they were!

There was a third man in the truck, nicknamed Molcajete because of his pockmarked complexion, who told them the immigration officers had made a mistake; he was an American citizen, born in San Benito. But he had no papers with him, and he understood some but spoke little English—he had worked in the fields ever since he was a little boy, and had never gone to school. He was thin and wiry, with dark brown skin, a broad nose that had probably been broken at least once, and short coarse black hair that seemed to stand on end, even though it was thoroughly slicked with brilliantine. They listened to his tale, commiserated with him, and urged him to talk to the officers; surely they would not deport a citizen!

The truck had gone south from the hospital, past the city cemetery, past the arroyo that ran through part of the town. There were few houses now, only freshly plowed fields that seemed to extend forever. One of the men in the group said the farmers were planting the cotton that would be picked in the summer. Finally they stopped at a long red brick building that had flags flying in front of it. There was a bus parked there also. The two officers opened the back doors and told the group to get out, then sent them to stand with a larger group that was assembled near the bus. Molcajete approached the officers and started to say something in broken English, but the officers were engrossed in their own conversation and would not listen.

Finally he yelled out, "Am americano! Americano de San Benito!"

One of the officers, the tallest one, turned around, and without skipping a beat said, "Sure, sure, Pancho. And I'm the king of England." His fellow officers laughed along with him.

Molcajete, frustrated, tried to hold the officer by the arm. The officer shook him off, and two others came over and grabbed Molcajete, pinning his arms back. The first officer came up to Molcajete, and in a voice that sounded more like a hiss than a whisper said, "You low-down piece of Mexican shit! I'll teach you to be grabbin' onto my arm." He balled his hands into fists, took aim, and punched twice, hard, in the stomach. Molcajete doubled over, gasping for air. The men who were holding him dragged him over to the group by the bus and dropped him to the ground unceremoniously, as one would drop a sack. They moved back to the group of officers.

The illegals stood quietly; no one moved, no one spoke, no one even breathed.

The tall officer took a couple of steps forward and addressed the group. "Well, we were gonna let you off in Noo-ay-vo La-ray-dough, but thanks to your amigo here, we're gonna take you all the way to See-you-dad War-az. Anybody got any objections?" Again, no one spoke. He grunted, "Huh, I thought as much." He turned to his fellow officers. "Jones! Let's get this show on the road."

Jones told the group to get into the bus. A couple of the men helped Molcajete to his feet and onto the bus with the others. They were boarded in groups of four, first four men, then four women, filling up the bus from the back, leaving the last four seats empty, and an empty row between each group of four. The officers were at the bus door, taking the names and places of birth from each as they boarded. Maria Dolores was with the last group to board; she wound up sitting right behind the metal cage barrier that separated them from the officers.

Once they were all in their seats and the barrier locked, the officers told them to open the windows, then got off the bus and went into the building, leaving one outside to guard the bus. He stood in the shade of the lone mesquite tree, watching both the road and the bus. Forty-five minutes later, three officers came out of the building and boarded the bus. One of them carried a folder with a sheaf of papers in it. The driver turned the ignition, it sputtered a bit then caught, and they took off.

The bus soon pulled up to a railroad crossing and stopped there. A freight train was coming towards them, slowing as it approached. The engineer stuck his head out the window and waved. The train came to a full stop, and the officers left the bus, walked up to one of the empty cars, and pulled open the door. The engineer met them there, and the officer handed him the folder with the papers.

They told the people to get off the bus, again in groups of four, and they were led to the freight car. Soon they were all settled in, the door was closed and locked, and the train started on its way again.

Once the train had started, Maria Dolores asked if anyone knew how far it was to Ciudad Juarez. Molcajete shook his head no. The officers had told the engineer that they were to be dropped off somewhere in the state of San Luis Potosí.

The only light in the car came from four small windows cut into the walls, about five feet up the sides. Maria Dolores could see the sky, and sometimes the tops of trees as they went by. As her eyes adjusted to the darkness, she made out a barrel standing in a corner, and a pail beside it. The barrel contained fresh water for drinking; the pail had been used as a makeshift toilet. Maria Dolores bundled up her shawl to use as a pillow and lay down, closing her eyes to the desperation in the faces of her companions.

When she woke up, it was dark. She had hoped it had been a nightmare, but quiet voices murmured in the blackness, telling her she was still on the train. The full reality of her situation hit her as she listened. One of the men was talking about his home in Veracruz, about the wife and children who depended on the money he sent every week. He had not even been paid for the last few days' work he had done in the field. One of the women said that she had left a three-year-old daughter and five year old twins in the care of her 10 year old daughter. Another woman spoke of her ailing husband, who could not work because of an injury sustained earlier in the year. The litany of laments continued long into the night, each adding to the sorrow felt by all.

The engineer finally let them off. Molcajete estimated they were about 10 miles south of San Luis Potosí. The group began walking north, as if it had been previously arranged. After half an hour, one of the men turned to the others and said they'd have a chance to hitch rides on the road, but only if they were in smaller groups, so they split up into groups of four. Maria Dolores walked with Molcajete and two of the women, Paula and Filomena. The women mentioned that they would be staying in San Luis; Filomena had relatives there who would help them out. Molcajete said he would walk back to the border if necessary. Maria Dolores asked if she could walk with him, and he agreed. The four kept a relatively fast pace and quickly outdistanced the rest of the group. When they reached the main road into San Luis Potosi, they walked a bit more slowly, and soon a truck picked them up and took them into the city.

They went to the home of Filomena's relatives, who fed them and invited them to spend the night there. The next day, Maria Dolores and Molcajete took off, heading for the border. They were able to hitch rides twice on the road; one got them to Ciudad Victoria, where they spent one night, and the other nearly to Matamoros. Molcajete had a few friends in Matamoros, and they went there when they entered the city. It took the friends a couple of days to arrange for a coyote to take both Maria Dolores and Molcajete across.

They reached Molcajete's home in San Benito at ten in the evening. As they approached, he ran ahead of Maria Dolores toward the gate of the crude fence that surrounded the yard. His family was sitting in the front yard, speaking in hushed tones. His mother saw him first, and let out a yell of relief. Molcajete ran into his mother's arms, and they both cried. The rest of the family came and surrounded them, all of them yelling and laughing at the same time. Each person had to touch him, hug him, kiss him.

Maria Dolores hung back in the shadows, watching the welcome. There must have been twenty people in the group. They made enough noise for five times that number. She turned to go, determined to find her way to Harlingen. She did not want to disturb the family. Molcajete saw her as she crept away, and called out to her. He quickly explained to his family that they had traveled together from San Luis, and that she was on her way to a job in Harlingen.

Molcajete's mother insisted that Maria Dolores spend the night with them. She promised to find a way for her to get to Harlingen the next day. She called out for her daughter Teresa to prepare some food for Molcajete and Maria Dolores; surely they must be hungry after their ordeal. Then she told Mario to get his guitar and play for them. Their sadness was ended, now they could celebrate. The traveling companions ate a meal of chilaquiles with coffee as the entire family joined in singing traditional Mexican ballads and corridos. They celebrated long into the night, finally calling it a night at around three in the morning.

The next day, they got one of the neighbors to take Maria Dolores to Harlingen. Maria Dolores thanked Molcajete and the driver and emerged from the old truck. She assured them that she would be all right. Then she turned toward the house and saw Marina standing at the door, holding the baby. The older woman pushed open the screen door and stepped out onto the red cement porch. She took two steps forward, allowing the door to slam behind her, then smiled broadly. "Bien venida a casa, Maria Dolores!"

When Paul came home that day, he was first angry with Marina for bringing one of those people into his house. But soon he realized that the baby would sleep in the room with the maid, and he and Marina would once again be able to sleep the whole night through together, so he didn't insist that she leave. After a while he seemed to grow used to the idea, though he never addressed the girl directly. Maria Dolores realized that the Señor did not like her, but it did not make a difference to her. When he was home, she stayed out of his way. Marina was just grateful that Paul hadn't made a fuss about it. She assumed he was accepting Maria Dolores.

14

Maria Dolores knelt in front of the picture of Our Lady of Guadalupe that graced the side altar at Immaculate Heart Church. "Cihuapili, Madre del Dios vivo, ¿cómo estas hoy? How are you? I come to ask you please to greet all my loved ones who have gone to your house in heaven…my mother and father, my husband, and my grandfather Diego. Tell them, if you please, that I am well. And that Violetita is well too. I am a little sad today, Madrecita, because el Señor Paul has decided to take his family to visit his mother up north. So I will not be able to celebrate the birth of our Lord with mijita. But there will be other years when we can celebrate together. But, Virgencita, we will be able to come here on your day. That will be good. I will see you then, here in this church. Cuida mis pasos al ir a casa. Guide my way home." She blessed herself and left the church.

15

Benita was rocking her baby girl, singing a lullaby.

"Su nana y su tata se fueron a León.

A ver el convite del burro pelón.

Ru, ru, fueron a León.

Ru, ru, burro pelón."

Toyita gurgled in her mother's arms, not at all interested in taking a nap.

"Duérmase, mi niña,

duérmase ya,

que ahi viene el viejo,

se la comerá."

The baby reached up and touched Benita's face softly. It seemed she could understand her mother's feelings, and return them. Benita had fallen in love with her when Doña Chucha first brought her into their lives, but she had not imagined that her love would grow so strong.

Some people say that you cannot love an adopted baby like you can your own, but that simply was not true. Don Lázaro, their landlord, had told her so. His wife, God rest her soul, had been a widow with two children when he married her. And he loved those two as much as the five they had brought into the world together. And he loved her daughter's children as well. Betty and Robertito were so cute.

Ah, well, her mind had wandered, and Victoria had fallen asleep all on her own. She set the baby down on the bed, surrounded her with pillows, and prepared lunch for her family.

She knew that their Christmas celebration was going to be a big one once again. Even though his wife had passed away, Don Lázaro was expecting his in-laws to come and prepare for the holidays as they had often done before. They would butcher a hog and make tamales and chicharrones in the big courtyard of the vecindad. The children would dress up as shepherds, and sing the Posadas at the different homes. Then they would all have a feast of tamales, chicharrones and champurrado. Benita had offered to make the champurrado this year, and Don Lázaro had gratefully accepted the offer. In the past, his wife had always made it.

Even though his wife had died in August, Don Lázaro was determined to make the Christmas as near to normal as possible for his children. He was proud that his daughters tried so hard to take over the responsibilities that their mother had handled with ease, but it also hurt that they should have to shoulder so much responsibility so soon. Benita knew this, and her heart went out to him and to his children. She had lost her mother when she was twelve, and she still felt the pain.

But now, her pain was less, because she had a little girl named after her mother. Victoria Ruiz was truly a blessing from God.

16

March 1951

Maria Dolores finished braiding Violeta's hair and turned her around. "¡Qué bonita mi muchachita! How pretty you look in your pink shorts and blouse! Now, go find your mother and tell her you are ready."

Violeta ran off, but was back before Maria Dolores had put away the brush and straightened the dresser. "Mama says you should come too, Nana Yolita."

"But why should I go, Violetita, if she is giving you your lessons!" Maria Dolores protested. She had been through this with Marina before. Marina insisted that Maria Dolores should learn to read and write, but Maria Dolores knew she would never be able to really speak the English, even though she could understand a fair amount now and say a few words.

"I don't know; she says she has a surprise for you. Come on, Nana, I don't want to keep Mama waiting." She took Maria Dolores's hand and led her to the dining room table.

Marina was sitting at the table, trying to suppress a grin. She held a little green book in her hand. "Mira esto. Look at this," she said as she handed the book to Maria Dolores. Maria Dolores opened it, saw by the pictures that it was upside down, giggled, then returned it to Marina.

"Es muy lindo," she said. "But what does it have to do with me?" She looked at Marina expectantly.

"Mrs. Lerma loaned this to me. It had belonged to her mother-in-law. Mira, Maria Dolores, es en español! It's a fourth-grade Spanish reader! Now you can learn to read and write in Spanish! And Violet will learn right along with you!"

Maria Dolores shook her head at this, but saw that there was no arguing with Marina. Once she had decided something, she would not change her mind. So by the end of the lesson, she could write her own name, as well as that of her daughter. She had also learned the Spanish alphabet, with its 30 letters. She diligently practiced them that night, and the next day was delighted to see that she could recognize and read them to Marina. Marina was so delighted that she took out her camera and took a picture of Maria Dolores and Violet sitting at the dining room table, studying their letters.

Marina felt very satisfied with herself. Maria Dolores would learn to read and write Spanish, then she would learn to speak and read and even write English. Then perhaps the girl would agree to approach INS about permanent residency…even citizenship. Oh, but she was getting ahead of herself again.

Of course, for now she wouldn't even mention it to Maria Dolores, because the girl was so frightened of the INS. Marina had never asked her exactly what happened when she was deported, but the few things that she had heard were not at all pleasant.

Molcajete had come by a few times in the first two years that Maria Dolores had been here, but she had always refused to go out with him. Finally, he had come and told her that he had met another girl, and that he was going to marry her. Maria Dolores had seemed relieved; later, she had confided to Marina that she had never thought of Molcajete that way. He had been a friend, someone who had passed a rough time with her, nothing more. Oh, he was a good man and all, and she was certain he would make a good husband for that girl. But he was not for Maria Dolores. In fact, nothing was more important to Maria Dolores than to care for Violetita, to be present for her and help in all that she could.

Marina often wondered how Maria Dolores could be so strong. She had promised that she would not tell Violetita that she was her real mother, and indeed had kept her promise. She always ceded authority to Marina and to Paul. She never betrayed in the slightest to Paul that her care for Violet was any more than that of a nanny. If Marina had any misgivings at all about bringing Maria Dolores into their household to care for Violet, if she had ever doubted that Maria Dolores could hold to her end of the bargain, the past four years had proven beyond a doubt that her trust and her faith were well placed. Maybe when Violet was older, when she could handle the truth, she and Maria Dolores would tell her the miraculous story of how their lives had been intertwined. But for now, they would continue as they were.

17

June 1951

Toyita was making mud cakes in the open area next to the shack they lived in. She had nearly emptied the canteen to make the mud, but now she was happily baking the cakes in the sun. She talked to her doll, Teresa, as she worked, telling her of the wonderful birthday party the doll was going to have, with all her friends there, and all the other people who made up Teresa's family. There was Chicho, the stray cat that always slinked into view when the Ruiz family was eating. And Quiqui, the cloth piglet that somebody had given Toya when she was a baby. And of course, there was Osito, the teddy bear that Don Lázaro had given Toyita.

Benita watched from the door as her daughter played. Toya had just celebrated her fourth birthday a few days before they left Harlingen, so the memory was fresh in her mind. Don Lázaro had attended, as had two of his granddaughters. Toyita had been very happy with her little party. Don Lázaro was holding their little home for them, but he had also planted a little seed in Benita's mind. Now that she was pregnant again, and would have three children, the rooms they rented from him were really not adequate. He suggested that they look into getting a place at Los Vecinos, the housing project across town. There, they could have a bedroom for the children and one for her and Beto. And they would also have a separate kitchen and living room. And even an indoor toilet. Since he worked for the City Waterworks, he got to see things all over town. He said the apartments there were nice, and reasonable for a family. She looked down at Toyita and made up her mind. As soon as they got back to Harlingen in November, they would go see about getting into Los Vecinos. But for now, she had better see about making lunch for her two Betos, who were working out in the field. She came out to the campfire near the shack, and as she bent over to place a pan on the grill, she felt a sharp pain. "Toya, ve a hablarle a tu papa. Ándale, dile que ya es tiempo."

Beto dropped everything as soon as he saw Toya running to get him. He had been expecting this. He told his son to go call Meli—Amelia Diaz Rivas, who often served as midwife among the migrants at that camp. He hurried home, where he found Benita lying down inside the shack. "I've sent for Amelia. 'Orita viene, Vieja. ¿Qué hago?" he panted.

"Put some water to boil, and take the clean white sheets out of the box. You know which one. And then, pos get out of the way until Meli tells you different." Beto quickly did as he was told. The water was boiling by the time the midwife arrived. She sent him packing, and told him to take the children with him. Matilde Araujo, another of the migrant women, had come to help.

Beto and his children walked to the edge of the field. He was nervous, but managed to entertain the children with talk of how they would live when they got back to Harlingen. Benita did not know this, but he had already gotten a space at Los Vecinos. His wife was not the only one who talked to Don Lázaro! So he told them about the apartment with two bedrooms and a bathroom with a tub and a toilet, inside the house! And he told them that there were many other children there that they could play with. And that there was a school nearby, where they would go (both children groaned at this), and they would learn many things.

Amelia performed her ministrations on Benita, and soon the younger woman was ready to give birth. Matilde assisted, watching carefully, for she too wanted to help other women through the labor, like Melita did. Within the hour, the child was born and cleaned off with olive oil bought especially for the birth. Amelia handed the baby to Benita, "Ten, tu Juanito tiene hambre."

"Mi Juanito? Es hombrecito?" Benita asked.

"Sí, muchacha, pos qué esperabas. Y es Juanito porque hoy es el mero día de San Juan!" Doña Amelia said firmly.

Benita smiled. "Yes, we will name him Juan, for his feast day. Please call Beto and the children."

Toyita was fascinated with her new brother. She was already planning to celebrate. This was even better than having a birthday party for Teresa. They would have a birthday party for Juanito! At four, she already knew that she would be a mommy someday. She told her mother so, "Voy a ayudarte con Juanito pa' praticar pa'cuando yo sea mama." She looked up at the ceiling. "I'm going to have nine baby boys and nine baby girls y vamos a tomar cafecito todos los días, como orita lo hago con Teresa y Osito y Quiqui."

18

April 1953

Paul got into his car, rolled down the window, and sat there for a short while. He'd just gotten news that he'd been waiting eight—no, nearly nine years to get. Every six months since he got here, he'd put in transfer requests, all denied, until now. And he had a new rank to boot. That was excellent news. Not that this particular transfer was savory—New Mexico—but at least he could get his family out of this hellhole.

The problem was—and he knew it would be a problem—he didn't want to take any excess baggage with him. Just his wife and daughter. But Marina would insist on bringing along that Mexican maid. Hell, she'd even been talking about trying to get papers for her. That'd never do. At times like this, he was tempted to follow his father's example and just put down his foot and say his way or the highway. His mom and all of the Henderson children had scars left over from when his dad put his foot down. But, he had sworn never to do that to his own wife, so that was out.

He chewed on his lower lip as he thought, then straightened up, turned the ignition key and shifted into gear. There was, by golly, one thing he could do. He drove down to the officer's club and went straight to the pay phone.

One short phone call later, and it was all set. All he had to do now was wait until after five, then go home. By then, it would be done, and all offices would be closed for the weekend…no chance of getting any information until it was too late. And of course, Monday would be moving day for them.

He arrived home at 5:30, only to find Marina in tears. A neighbor told her what had happened. Maria Dolores had had the presence of mind to take Violet to the neighbor's house when the INS came and picked her up. He was very understanding of Marina's pain, even to the point of being apologetic about the transfer. But he explained patiently that he could not ask to delay the transfer; that just wasn't done in the military. He suggested that she leave word with that Maggie or Margie or Margarita, whatever her name was, so that if—when Maria Dolores came back, there would be a message for her. Marina had been so hopeful about that!

Of course, he could fix it so that no news of that girl ever reached his wife.

19

October 1953

Maria Dolores sighed heavily as she ironed another pair of blue jeans. It had been six months since that awful day, right before Violetita's sixth birthday, when she'd been picked up by la migra and deported. This time she'd been taken to the southernmost region of Mexico, and it had taken her four months to get back to the Valley. But when she arrived, she'd found that Marina and Violetita were gone. Marina had left her a note with Margarita Torres, promising to write and send for her. But since they'd left, not one letter had arrived. Maria Dolores had been back two months; it had been nearly six and a half since the Hendersons had moved away.

Margarita wiped her forehead with the cloth diaper she always wore on her shoulder. "Ay, Maria Dolores, it is time to stop waiting for the letter that will never arrive. Mira, I know that Marina is a good person…pero that husband of hers probablemente does not let her write to us! You know how he is…and, pos, es el marido; he is the husband." As she spoke, Margarita waved her hands about, gesturing as if to emphasize her words.

Four-year-old Mandito, her youngest, now stood a bit behind her and mimicked her gestures perfectly. Margarita noticed Maria Dolores looking behind her and turned around to see what she was looking at. "Mandito! Qu'estas haciendo, güerco! Métete pa'dentro. Andale." She shrieked at the boy, then laughed as he ran inside, letting the screen door slam behind him. She was laughing so hard that tears streamed down her face. When she did not stop, Maria Dolores turned off the iron and went over to her. Margarita was sobbing now. "Mandito is four years old now, almost five. In another year he will start school, like his brothers. I thought…I mean, the four of them, they are all two years apart. I thought Mandito was the last one. But now I am expecting again. Ay, Maria Dolores. I am going to have another. Maybe this time God will give me a little girl."

Margarita's tears had subsided; her eyes were shining brightly. "You know, I never said anything to Marina, but I always wanted a little girl like her Violet. She learned Spanish so well, que hasta parecía Mexicana. She seemed like one of us." She looked at Maria Dolores now. "Yolita, I cannot pay you any more. Yo sé que no es mucho lo que te doy, but I cannot do it any more. I have to save, for when the baby is born." She blew her nose on a white handkerchief and stood up.

"Pero mira," she continued, "have you ever been to Los Vecinos? It is a government housing project, and I made an application for you to live there. Mi concuña Aida tiene un ahijado, y su novia trabaja con la ciudad. Your application to live there is already approved."

"Application? Los Vecinos? Dónde está eso?" Tears sprang to Maria Dolores's eyes as she spoke. The more she moved, the less likely any letter from Marina would reach her. But she knew she could no longer impose on Margarita and her family. "When do I leave?"

"Los Vecinos is near Assumption Church. Anda, mira, vas a estar cerquita de la iglesia. You can go todos los días si quieres. And if you get a letter de Marina, pos we will take it to you! You know we will. Ya verás que you are going to be happy there!"

20

Marina gave Paul another letter to send to Margarita and Maria Dolores. "I don't know why you keep writing to those people," he said. "They've never answered any of your other letters, have they? You know, they're just not like us, Marina." He rubbed her shoulders tenderly as he spoke. "They tend to stick pretty much to their own. They prob'ly just didn't know how to tell you, you know, that this friendship wouldn't last any longer. And as for that girl. Well, she's prob'ly in Mexico or something. After all, that's where she really belongs. I mean, I know you really liked her and all, but she was an alien, and she didn't have any papers. There's probably no way she came back to this country. She prob'ly went and found her own people or something. You should give up on it already."

Marina didn't answer, just held the letter in front of him, waiting for him to take it. He plucked it out of her hand angrily. "All right, all right. I'll take it. But I just don't see why you're so insistent." He walked out of the small apartment on base that the Air Force had provided for them.

Paul got into the car and drove off. He wished he could convince

Marina that there was just no use in trying to contact those people, but she'd never let go if he didn't take matters into his own hands. So this letter would go into file 13 right along with the others she'd given him. No, on second thought…he had a friend who worked at the base post office. Maybe…yeah, he could get this letter stamped "Return to Sender, Addressee Unknown." That would end it once and for all. Then he wouldn't have to worry anymore, and could even get Marina into some off-base housing. She'd been asking since they got here, but he'd put her off, because then she might send a letter herself. But if she became convinced that there was no way to get through, well, that would make life much easier.

Ten days later, he walked into the apartment with sad news for Marina. She looked at the envelope and started crying. He put his arms around her and consoled her. "It's okay, Honey. We really can get along without her, you know. I mean, you're so good with Violet, and she's doing well here, isn't she?"

Marina sobbed. "Oh, Paul, you just don't understand. I really miss Maria Dolores. It wasn't just the help she gave me."

Violet walked in and saw her mother crying. "Mama, what's wrong? Are you sick? Did something happen?" She turned to her father. "Daddy, why is Mommy crying? Make her stop crying, please. I don't like it when she cries!" Paul and Marina both hugged Violet.

"It's nothing, really, Violet. Mommy just misses Nana Yolita very much, and now we don't know how to contact her. That's all. I think that the Torres must have moved away or something. That's all." Paul patted Violet's back as he said this. Marina dried her tears with Paul's handkerchief and smiled. She knelt beside Violet. "See? I've stopped crying now. I'm all right. We'll be all right." She hugged her daughter once again.

Violet kissed her mother's hand and said, "Oh, Mommy, wait till you see what we did in school today! First grade is so exciting. Although, of course, I already know how to read and write my name, because you taught me and Maria Dolores, remember? Well, anyway, we got to go to the library, and I picked a book to read, and Mrs. Hill, the library lady, she told me that this book was for third graders, not for me, because it was too hard, and then my teacher, she came over and told Mrs. Hill that no, that I could read that book because I already knew how to read. And you know what? Here it is! It's about this girl named Rebecca and she lives at Sunnybrook Farm, Mommy. See? And I can read it! You wanna see? You want me to read to you?" Violet always—almost always—spoke in a torrent, as though she would be interrupted if she didn't run all her words together. Marina told her to save the book until before bedtime, and she would listen to her read then. Right now, it was time to prepare supper for the family.

Marina didn't see Paul's smile, or she might have questioned him. And when he knelt down and told her and their daughter that he had found a house to rent in town, she was so happy that she didn't think it odd that he'd find a house now, when he couldn't find one just last week. She'd never liked base housing, because it meant that the only people they met were Air Force. She wanted to get to know what the "real" people were like, wanted to get a true sense of place wherever they went.

Paul had selected a lily-white neighborhood, or so he thought. It was true that the neighbors on their block were all white, but across the alley, on the next block, there were several Indian families, and some Mexican families too. Albuquerque was probably just as segregated as the rest of the country, but it so happened that they were on the boundary line between two neighborhoods. So, the Hendersons actually had the best of both worlds, because most of their white neighbors also made friends with the neighbors behind them.

The day after they moved into the neighborhood, Marina and Violet walked to the elementary school that was only two blocks away. They enrolled Violet, and she entered first grade there. As soon as she walked into her new classroom, two little girls said hello and asked her name. She'd obviously found new friends already. Marina left, and decided to explore the neighborhood for a bit before going home.

FOUR

The Lady and the old man walked down the mountain slowly, as if enjoying the sounds of nature, the fragrance of the flowers. As always, they seemed to communicate without words. They walked to the area where the village had once stood. Nature was reclaiming the area, though a few stalks of maize still grew among the native plants.

The two walked to the riverbank and saw how clear the water was running. It would serve the people in the city at the foot of the mountain well.

The Lady found a boulder and sat there, holding a blue stone in her hands. The old man sat at her feet and touched the stone. He gently brought it to his face. He spoke to it quietly, the sounds no more than a murmur. Then he gave it back to the Lady. She held the stone close to her heart for a moment, then set it down again, this time next to a smaller blue stone. She gave them both a gentle push, and they began a tandem roll.

The old man looked at the stones for a while, then turned and took the Lady's hand. They walked toward the top of the mountain together.

21

November 1953

Maria Dolores entered the church and quietly closed the door behind her. The church was warm, even though the heaters were not on; the candles flickering in front of the picture of the Virgen de Guadalupe and the statue of the Sacred Heart of Jesus provided heat and light.

She went up to the altar railing and knelt. "Buenas tardes, Señor. I thank you for this day. And I just want to greet you, but I am going to talk to your mother. You see, being a mother, she understands more than the words I can say to her. You understand, don't you?" With that, she got up and walked over to the picture of the Virgen de Guadalupe. She touched the frame lovingly before kneeling. "Madrecita, ¿cómo estas ahora? I know I did not come this morning because I went to help Margarita with the children. She is having a lot of the morning sickness, and she does not feel very well. Please take care of her and of her baby. And I hope it is a little girl, because Margarita wants one so much. She is a good mother, and a little girl would be perfect for her.

"And, Virgencita, please also take care of mijita Violetita, and of Marina too. Margarita says that I should just forget them, and make a life for myself. But Margarita does not know that Violetita is my daughter. How does one forget a child? You are a mother. You know it is impossible." She wiped the tears that had welled in her eyes. "I know that Marina is taking good care of Violetita, for she is a mother to her. I know also that you watch over both of them. I just wish…. no, that is not right, is it? I must wish for the will of God, and for the patience to accept it.

"Also, Madre mía, I want to give you thanks. Now I have four houses to clean every week. I don't understand how people can need help to clean their homes, but I am grateful that they do. Bueno, es todo por ahora. I will come back tomorrow afternoon, after I have finished cleaning the house of the Richards. They are very nice, especially la Señora. I will tell you about them tomorrow. Buenas tardes, Señora, and thanks."

Maria Dolores stood up, walked to the entrance of the church, and blessed herself at the holy water font there. Then she wrapped her rebozo tightly around herself and walked out, going down the street beside the church until she was directly across from the entrance to her block at Los Vecinos. As she crossed M Street, she espied a little girl with black pigtails playing jump rope near her apartment. Maria Dolores gave a start…the little girl looked so familiar…. she called out "Violetita! Mi Violeta!" but the little girl did not even turn. Puzzled, Maria Dolores approached the child. It was Violeta! But what was she doing here, dressed like that? She touched the little girl's hair. "Violeta? Dónde está tu mamá?"

The little girl turned to face her. "Yo no me llamo asina. Soy Toya…Victoria. Mi mami 'ta allá en la casa. 'Tan despacando." She pointed to the apartment across the patio from Maria Dolores's home. "Tu vives aquí? Cómo te llamas? No 'tavas aquí antes."

Maria Dolores knelt in front of Toya, studying her face. No, this little girl did not have a birthmark near her left eye, as Violeta did. But otherwise she was exactly like her daughter. How could this be? "I am Maria Dolores, and I live there, in number 12. What is your mother's name, Toya?"

"*Benita, Benita Ruiz. Y mi papi es Beto. El 'ta muy grandote. Mi mami 'ta más chiquita que mi papi. Pero ella sabe hacer de comer. Tu también sabes hacer de comer? Yo tengo hambre pero mi mami 'ta despacando y no puede hacer de comer.*"

("Benita, Benita Ruiz. And my daddy is Beto. He's real big. My mommy's smaller than my daddy. But she knows how to prepare food. Do you know how to prepare food too? I'm hungry but my mommy's unpacking and she can't make lunch now.")

Toya talked as much as her Violeta did.

"Yes, Toya, I know how to cook. And I'll tell you what. Do you like migas?" The little girl nodded. "Good. Why don't I make some migas for all of your family so you can eat? How many are you? Do you have brothers and sisters?"

"*Tengo dos hermanos, Betito y Juanito. Betito tiene 8 años, y Juanito tiene 2. Yo tengo 6 años, y dice mami que me va a meter a la 'scuela; yo no quiero ir porque todos hablan inglés y yo no. Yo hablo puro 'spañol porque soy purita mexicana. Asina dice mi papi. Mmmm y sí me gustan las migas, pero no con chile, porque pica. Vas a hacer migas sin chile o con chile?*"

"*Te las hago sin chile para tí, y con chile para tus papás. 'Ta bueno?*"

("I have 2 brothers, Betito and Juanito. Betito is 8 years old, and Juanito is 2. I am 6 years old, and mommy says she's gonna put me in school; I don't want to go because everybody talks English and I don't. I speak only Spanish because I'm pure Mexican. That's what my daddy says. Mmmm, and I do like migas, but not with chili, because it burns. Are you going to make migas with chili or without?"

"I'll make them without chili for you and with chili for your parents. OK?")

"'Ta güeno. Asina sí." Toya laughed and twirled as she did.

"Bueno, ya me voy. Dile a tu mami que no se vaya a preocupar. Yo les voy a hacer de cenar. Tell your mother that I will make supper for your family. I will call you when it is ready."

22

Maria Dolores walked on to her apartment and set about cutting corn tortillas, onions, tomatoes, and serrano peppers to make the migas. She wondered about the miracle God had brought about in her life. She did not have her Violetita now, but there was this child who looked so much like her daughter that she could gauge her own daughter's growth by Victoria's. She thanked her Virgen de Guadalupe as she prepared the meal. She made a pot of coffee and heated milk and sugar to mix with it, served it into the six mugs, then stepped out to the patio and called out to the family to come in.

Toya ran to her apartment, followed by her older brother, who carried the two-year-old. Benita and Beto came up more slowly. They were obviously apenados about coming to eat supper in her home. "I know what it is to move in," she said. "I just moved in three weeks ago. I was so hungry by the time we finished that I could have eaten a piece of carton, if it had salsa on it! But my friend, Margarita, had some tacos, and shared them with me. Por eso, I decided to share with you. Andale, come in. Aquí tienen su pobre casa." She held the screen door open for them to enter.

Benita walked in first, followed by Beto. The living room was sparsely furnished; it had two chairs and a small table between them. There was an ojo de Dios on the wall, with the picture of Our Lady of Guadalupe centered on it. The dining room adjoined the living room, and was furnished with a small table with four chairs, which were the same as the two in the living room. The dining table had a beautiful embroidered tablecloth on it. Off to one side of the dining room was the kitchen, which was standard for the projects. It had a small white stove and a small refrigerator. The double sink was of white porcelain, and the countertops were yellow. The walls and cabinets were yellow also. A door at the rear of the dining room led to a short hall, which ran to the back door. Along the hall were two doors; one led to the single bedroom and one to the bathroom. Maria Dolores lived in a one-story, one-bedroom apartment flanked on each side by two-story, two-bedroom apartments reserved for families with one to three children. The Ruizes were moving into a two-story apartment with three bedrooms across the patio. Benita was pregnant with their fourth child, due in January.

As they entered the dining room, Benita offered to help Maria Dolores, but she told them to sit down and relax, the meal was ready to be served. She brought out a stack of flour tortillas and two frying pans filled with migas. Six Mexican clay mugs filled with hot cafe con leche sat on the table already. Maria Dolores gave one to each of the children, along with a taco de migas, and told them to sit in the living room. "Es que nomás tengo tres platos," she explained to the parents. "I don't usually have company, unless Margarita comes with her son Mandito. But maybe now that I have new friends, I will get more plates." She smiled at the two, who were already filling their plates with the tasty food.

Benita was almost as talkative as her daughter. She quickly set the pace for the conversation, comparing the weather in Washington state to the weather in the Valley, commenting on the long journey from los trabajos back home, even expressing hope that Victoria would like school, because Betito seemed to be having some trouble keeping up. She wished that they could come back earlier, so her children could start school in September, but if they left early, the patrones would not hire them the next year, and how would they live then? "Ay," she said, "the life of the migrante is hard, pero ni modo, si para trabajar nacimos. Verdad, Viejo? We were born to work."

Beto swallowed the forkful of migas he had just shoveled into his mouth. "Bueno, Vieja…no para trabajar…but to eat, yes—y si we want to comer, pos hay que trabajar! Y también si queremos tener hijos," he laughed. Beto was not tall, but he was heavyset, with a big round stomach, which he rubbed as he spoke. His eyes twinkled at Benita, who blushed as he spoke about having children. "Don't be embarrassed, Vieja. Al cabo que estamos casados por las tres leyes!"

"What three laws? We're married by the law of God and the law of the state." Benita scolded. "What is the third law?"

"Pos, the law of love, mi amor. Que no? Else we wouldn't have all these children."

"Sabes que? You and your ley del amor can go finish unpacking. I will help Maria Dolores clean up here. Ándale." Benita opened the door for her husband and shooed him out. "Don't pay attention to him, Maria Dolores. He is always playing around. But he is a good husband and father. And, to tell the truth, I do love him." They both laughed heartily. The two women walked into the kitchen and cleaned it thoroughly.

23

March 1955

Maria Dolores knocked on Benita's door. She had stopped at Lara's Bakery after work, and bought some pan dulce for the merienda. She probably shouldn't have, for Mrs. Garza had just told her she would not need her any more. The children were all in school now, and she could handle the housework by herself. Now Maria Dolores had only two houses to clean, because Mr. and Mrs. Richards had moved to San Antonio. Mrs. Richards wanted her to go along, but she could not leave the Valley. Well, she thought, la Virgencita has never failed me. Something will come up.

Benita opened the door wide and let her in. "Come in. I have just given Juanito a bath right now, and he is putting on his clothes. He went and got himself all dirty playing wrestling with the older boys. You should have seen him! Grass stains on his clothes, and at least three dirt rings on his skinny neck." She noticed the bag in Maria Dolores' hand. "Oh, you have sweet bread! Let me make some coffee right away. Ándale, Juanito!

Apúrale que aquí está Maria Dolores! Come say hello to her." She walked into the kitchen as she said this. Then she looked at Maria Dolores' face. "Muchacha! What is the matter? You look like you've lost your best friend."

When Maria Dolores told her about Mrs. Garza and Mrs. Richards, Benita said, "Do not worry about it. We are going up north in two weeks. Why don't you go with us? You didn't want to go last summer, but you were working every day then. But now, two houses are not enough to buy food, much less pay the rent and the utilities. Mira, here, they will hold your apartment for you until you come back. And you can make enough money in the summer to at least pay rent for the year, plus. Then you can live with only 2 houses to clean each week. What do you say?"

Maria Dolores looked at Benita. Here was the solution she had asked la Virgen for! "Yes, Benita, I will go, if you will have me. Thank you!" The door slammed just then, and both women looked up to see Toya crying her heart out. "Toyita! Que te pasa, Niña?" Maria Dolores had become very close to the little girl, who had grown at least four inches in the last year and a half.

"I had a fight with Soila Treviño. She called me 'la hija del lechero'— the milkman's daughter—because my whole family is dark-skinned, and I am not. Mami, she said that means that I'm not my father's child. Her mother says you must have had a gringo to have a daughter like me! What does it mean, Mami? I did not like the way she said it." Toya's sobs had wound down, but she was still crying. "Pero no me dejé. I pulled Soila's hair and scratched her face." Benita wrapped her daughter in her arms and smoothed her hair, trying to calm her. "Mami," she sobbed, "why am I different? Why don't I look like my brothers?"

"Mija, te voy a decir una historia that is true. When your brother Betito was eighteen months old, Doña Chucha la partera, the midwife, brought a beautiful baby girl to me, a baby whose mama had died in childbirth. Doña Chucha knew that I was still breast-feeding Betito, and that I had plenty of milk to offer this baby. When I saw the baby girl, I fell in love with you, and immediately said yes. Your father also fell in love with you when he saw you. It was the end of April, and Doña Chucha said you were one week old. That is why we celebrate your birthday on April 23."

"I am not your daughter, Mami? I don't have a mother or a father?" Toya was sobbing once again, so frightened at the possibility.

"Mijita, you are ours, as surely as if I had carried you inside me. You are a special blessing from God. I gave you my mother's name, Victoria, so that you would truly be mine. Ya ves, you are the only daughter I ever did have. All our other children are boys." Benita kissed her daughter's tears away. "Nobody can say you are not my daughter, or that Beto is not your father. And if Soila tells you anything, ever again, you tell her that Diosito la va a castigar si anda hablando mal de otra gente. Tell her she better go to confession to the priest." Toya smiled tentatively, then laughed outright at the thought of sending Soila to the priest.

Maria Dolores had sat silently during the entire exchange. Could it be possible, she wondered. Could this little girl also be her daughter? But how? She tried to remember the events of that day, almost eight years ago, when she had gone to Doña Chucha's to give birth. She remembered the pain, then waking up in the hospital. By that time, Violetita had already been born. It had never occurred to her that she could have had twins that day. She had to find out. Perhaps…it could not be possible. Could it?

"…verdad, Maria Dolores?" Benita was speaking, but Maria Dolores had not heard a word. She looked at her friend. "Le digo a Toya que tú vas al norte con nosotros este año." Benita repeated.

"Oh, Maria Dolores! If you go with us, I will be so happy! I don't know why, but I love you very much. It's like…it's like I knew you all my life, but you weren't here before. You know what I mean?" Toya rattled on happily, her recent grief all but forgotten.

Maria Dolores gave her a fierce hug, then got up to leave. She told

Benita that she had much to do at home, and that she would be back tomorrow afternoon. Benita looked at her strangely, but nodded her assent.

24

Maria Dolores went to Doña Chucha's house. She had not been there since that day nearly eight years ago. A young man came to the door when she knocked. There was a brief flare of recognition in his eyes when he saw her. "I am looking for Doña Chucha," she said.

"My grandmother died three years ago," he replied. "What is it you want?"

"You know who I am." It was not a question.

"I know. After you, my grandmother was not the same; she was afraid always, afraid the police would come after her." He looked at her. "We thought you had died."

"What happened to my baby?" Maria Dolores figured that question would be better. If there had not been another baby, he could deny it. But if there had been, he would tell her. "What happened to my little girl?" Tears had sprung into her eyes. "Please tell me the truth."

"My grandmother gave her to a family that lived down the street. They had another baby…. and, well, she thought they could take care of her. They did accept her."

"Do you remember their name? Who was this family?" she asked, though she already knew the answer to that.

"I don't remember exactly…It was Reyes or Rios or Ruiz. Something like that. I'm not sure. But the lady was Benita, I know that." Maria Dolores had turned around and started walking away. "Hey," he called out. "She didn't know you were alive. You never came back. She waited a week."

She had been walking for maybe twenty minutes when she looked up. She was standing in front of Immaculate Heart of Mary Church, where she had spent so much time during her pregnancy. She entered and found the statue of La Virgen de Guadalupe. She fell to her knees and cried. No words would come; no prayer seemed sufficient. Then she felt a hand on her shoulder, soft and gentle. "Sometimes it helps if we talk to someone, unburden ourselves," the priest said softly. She looked at him, startled. "I'm Father Mike. We can talk in the chapel in the rectory, if you like. It can be under the seal of confession. No one else need know." He helped her up, and led the way to the rectory.

For the first time since she had talked to Evita, Maria Dolores told her life's story, from her grandfather's death to the rape to the discovery that Toyita was her daughter, a daughter she did not even know existed. She talked until she was exhausted, and still she continued, until everything had been said, until she could say no more. All her confusion, all her pain came out. The priest gently prodded at times, asked a few questions, but most of all he listened, listened with patience and understanding, even though her story was almost beyond belief.

When she finished, he allowed her to sit in silence for a long while, giving time for her spirit to be at rest again. Then, quietly, he asked, "Maria Dolores, what do you want for yourself, for your daughter? Do you want to claim your daughter? Do you want her to live with you? Do you want to have her live with Benita? Do you want to raise her yourself? Do you want to help raise her? My child, what you decide will affect many lives.

Take your time in deciding, but you must decide before you go back and see them again. What you do must be done with conviction, and not just because it came out without thinking."

Fr. Mike left her in the chapel and went to the church to pray before the Blessed Sacrament. When he first came to this parish three years ago, he had heard the midwife's final confession. Of all the things she had confessed, this one thing had weighed most heavily on her conscience. She had failed the young girl by putting her out on the sidewalk at the first hint of trouble, then had lied to the couple she took the baby to. "Lord God, help me to help this young woman. Give me the wisdom to guide her so that no harm comes to her or her daughter. Amen." He blessed himself, and returned to the rectory. He was surprised to find Maria Dolores sitting in his office, dry-eyed and calm.

"Padre, I have made my decision. I think it is best for my daughter, and I hope that Benita will agree with me. Toyita knows she is adopted, but she thinks her mother is dead. Benita loves Toya with all her heart. I too love my daughter; I loved her even before I knew she was my daughter. Toyita is too young, I think, to face another surprise. I don't think I should tell her the truth just yet. Benita is a very good mother, not only to my Toyita, but to her sons as well. I will tell Benita my story without talking about Toya, and if she does not see that Toyita is my daughter, then I will explain it to her. But I want only the chance to help her family, and to see my daughter grow up. It is hard enough that I lost Violetita. I do not want to lose Toyita too."

Maria Dolores looked up and saw relief on the priest's face. She smiled slightly. "I want what is best for my daughter, Padre. I will do all in my power to protect her." She stood up. "But if Benita does not want to listen to me, may I come to you for help? Will you talk to her?"

Father Mike nodded. He walked with her to the door as she left.

25

It was not quite two o'clock when Maria Dolores arrived at Los Vecinos. She knocked on Benita's door, and Beto answered. "Pásale, Yolihuani. Benita will be right back. She just put Juanito to sleep. Pásale." He saw the look on her face. "Is something the matter? You look very pale."

"No, Beto. It's just...I have to talk to you and Benita. Alone." She entered and sat at the dining table. Beto called Benita, and she came downstairs immediately.

"Maria Dolores, ¿qué pasa? What do you need to talk about? Apoco you found a boyfriend?" Benita always joked with Maria Dolores about getting married.

"No, Benita, I have not found a boyfriend. But I...can we all sit down?" Beto and Benita sat at the dining table with her. She started again. "I told you about my family and how they died. But I have not told you everything that happened in my life. Yesterday, when Toyita came crying and told you what had happened, and then you told her how you had adopted her, I knew I had to find out the truth. Yesterday, when I left here, I went to—No, let me start with what happened to me in September of 1947."

Benita and Beto listened intently as she told the entire story, including her visits with Doña Chucha's grandson and with the priest at Immaculate Heart. "I do not want to take your daughter away from you. But I do want to be close to her, to help her grow up. Please. I lost my other daughter. Let me help you with Victoria." She looked at Benita, then at Beto.

They were stupefied. Benita was crying, as much for Maria Dolores as for herself and Toyita. She stood up and went to embrace Maria Dolores. Beto seconded her action. "Maria Dolores, we always felt that there was something special about you. The way Toyita took to you, and Betito and Juanito too. We cannot imagine our life without you. Now more than ever, you must come with us up north, and be part of our family all year long."

Maria Dolores accepted their love and their invitation. "Please believe that I will never tell her anything." Benita was shaking her head at this.

"No, Maria Dolores. When Victoria is old enough to hear the truth and understand it, we will tell her. We will tell her together." Benita looked at her husband, and he nodded in agreement.

Juanito called down from the bedroom, insisting that he was thirsty. The three downstairs called back, telling him to go back to sleep. Then Beto shook his head, went and poured a glass of water and hurried up the stairs to his son. Benita and Maria Dolores made plans for the trip up north, and Victoria found them there when she came home from school.

As usual, she regaled them with tales from school. Andrés el Gordo had fallen in love with skinny Rebeca, and kept giving her candies, which she generously shared with all her friends. Rebeca didn't really like him, but the candies were really good, Hershey's chocolate, because his uncle had a *tiendita* where he sold candies and school supplies, so Andrés had an almost endless supply. So, naturally, Rebeca accepted the candies. Who wouldn't? *El malinche de* Mario imitated the teacher, who had a habit of walking to the cloakroom and blowing her nose in there, as if the children could not hear. But Mario made it sound more like a fart than blowing his nose. And then of course there was the *chocante de* Cipriana, who called herself "Cissy" *y se creía muy gringa*, y she would never, ever talk to you in Spanish. No, because she was American...su mamá and su papá had both been born aquí en Harlingen, *y los dos hablan* perfect Inglich. *Sí, tu....le hacen permanente para que tenga* curly hair like *las gringas en las* movies. *Y* they never go *al Teatro Azteca ni al Teatro Grande*...oh, no. They go to the Arcadia and to the Rialto, *porque* there the movies are in Inglich."

Toyita put one hand on her hip and the other behind her head. "*Y* you should see, Maria Dolores, how she *se monea, como si fuera* a teenager. *Y nunca usa trensas, porque pos 'nomás las* poor Mexicans *usan* braids.'" She grabbed hold of her own braids and held them out and up. Her eyes lit up in a laugh. "*Y lo más* funny *es que, pos 'ta bien prieta...más* dark que Juanito!" Toya shrugged and crossed her arms over her chest. "*Fíjate nomás.*"

The entire family was laughing so hard that tears squeezed out of their eyes.

26

April 1955

Marina and Violet were sitting at the dining room table, filling out
invitations to her eighth birthday party. Though her birthday was actually
on Friday, the party would be on Saturday afternoon. Violet had wanted
a piñata, but her father had vetoed that idea, so they had hired a clown to
entertain the guests. Marina had taken Violet to the drugstore, and they
had found invitations with a clown on the front. Violet was allowed to
invite ten girls, which was fine with her, because there were eight girls in
her class, and she could also invite Betty and Marcie, who were only six,
but who lived next door and were really nice anyway.

Paul was working late that evening, so Marina and Violet had eaten a
light supper after the little girl had finished her homework. Then they had
worked on the invitations, and had laid them out on the table, to give the
India ink time to dry. Violet had taken her bath and fallen asleep by the
time Paul got home.

Marina knew Paul had his supper on the base, so she asked if he'd like a glass of tea, or a beer. He agreed to the beer, so they were walking into the kitchen together when the invitations caught his eye. He started reading the names on the envelopes. "Marcie and Betty Murchison, Patsy Moore, Lila Childress, Betty Burroughs, Susie Quentin, Clara Bighorn, Candace Fellsworth, Janie Chapman, and Nancy Romero. Whoa, wait a minute! Clara Bighorn and Nancy Romero? Aren't those names Indian? I don't want no Indian kids here when I'm home. You know that, Marina. It's bad enough I have to stand 'em at the base. I won't have 'em here too. Now, I wish you wouldn't mix with them either, but I let you do what you want when you're on your own. But I won't have them at this party." He saw the look on Marina's face. "And no, I'm not going anywhere on Saturday. It's my day off, and I plan to be here…besides, my little girl is turning eight, and her daddy's throwing her a party. And that's that!" He took those two invitations out and tore them into tiny pieces. He grabbed the bottle of beer from Marina's hand and stomped off into the living room, flicked on the television set and sat down.

He took a couple of swallows, looked at the bottle, then took a couple more. "And I'll tell you something else," he said, his voice a bit louder now. "I don't want my little girl mixing with them Indians. It's bad enough we had that damn maid that you called a nanny for so long. Humph! At least she had her usefulness." His voice grew louder still. "But mixing just gives the kid ideas about what's right and wrong. I tell you, whites gotta stick with whites. And that's that!" He finished off his beer and set the bottle down defiantly.

From the bedroom, Violet called out sleepily, "Momma? Is something the matter? Are you okay?"

"Everything's just fine, Sweetheart," Marina sang out. "It's just that your daddy and I forgot ourselves and raised the volume on the television set. Go back to sleep, baby." She turned to Paul and whispered fiercely, "You see! Keep your voice down. You don't want Violet to hear us fighting, do you?"

Paul's voice was subdued. "No, no I don't. But I also don't want her to have those Indians here. There's just no two ways about it, Marina. I don't like Indians. I never have and I never will. There's no use in my getting to know them, or spending time with them, or anything like that. You may not agree with me, you may think I'm wrong, but I know I will never like an Indian. Or a Mexican for that matter. Now, I know they're in this country whether I like it or not, and maybe they even got a right to, I don't know. I'm not arguing that at all. But I do not have to mix with them. And I won't. Period." He looked at her, expecting a response, hoping he wouldn't get one.

Marina sat silent for a long time, stung by the vehemence with which he'd said all that. A war raged inside her. Paul could be so sweet, so loving. He'd been a model father for Violet, even helping to select her wardrobe, and bandaging some of the various cuts and scrapes she'd experienced through the years. Deep inside he was a really good man, but his father had filled his head with so many wrong ideas about people, always emphasizing the differences between him and others instead of the things they had in common. His father had been a violent man, often beating his son and his wife. It was a miracle that Paul had not grown up into a wife-beater. But in fact he hadn't. If only he had also rejected his father's ideas about people. Unfortunately, his mother had shared those ideas, so Paul accepted them without question.

That was why she had never told him the truth about Violet's parentage. She had been afraid he would reject the baby she wanted so much. But now, there was no doubt in her mind that he loved his daughter. He'd just made that comment about daddy's little girl. Maybe if he realized that he not only loved her but liked her as well, and she was both Mexican and Indian to boot, maybe then he'd realize that there's really more in common among people than different between them. Maybe she should tell him the truth about Violet. Maybe that would be the best thing to do.

She looked over at her husband. He didn't look as tense as he did just a few minutes ago. "Paul?" She said tentatively. He looked at her. "Paul, you do love Violet, don't you?"

"Yes, I love her. That's why I'm telling you…"

"Paul," she interrupted. "What if I told you that her mother was Indian? Or Mexican?" She tried to gauge his reaction, but his face was blank. "Or both? What if you knew that your daughter was Mexican Indian?" She waited for his reaction.

For a long time, he said nothing. His jaw clenched and unclenched several times, and he was trembling slightly, his entire body on edge. He just couldn't…it wasn't possible. He looked at his wife again. No, there was truth in those eyes. He took three deep breaths. And comprehension came to his face. "It was that maid, wasn't it? She was the mother? How convenient for her to just have a kid, then come back and help raise it without having any of the financial burden. Hell, even to get paid for doing it. And you provided the fool who could…does she know? Violet. Does she know what she is?"

Marina had lost all color from her face, and she had started trembling too. "No. She doesn't even know she's adopted. Remember? Even her birth certificate…"

"Says you and I are the parents. I'd forgotten." He put his face very close to hers and whispered, "Well, you make sure she never knows."

He straightened to full height. "I'll finish doing my job with her, but I don't want her throwing it in my face like you just did. I don't know how you could have done this to me, Marina. I have loved you and I have loved you well. Right now I don't know how I feel."

He turned and walked to the front door. "I know I can't sleep here tonight. I'm going to the base. We can talk in the morning." He walked out, closing the door softly behind him.

Marina went to the dining room table and looked at the invitations still spread out there. Tears plopped on them as she tried to gather them; her hands seemed separate from her body and wouldn't do exactly as she wanted. Finally, the ink had run on most of the envelopes, so she just threw them all in the trashcan. She turned off the light in the dining room, locked the front door, and just sat on the sofa. She didn't think she would sleep at all that night.

27

She opened her eyes the next morning to find her daughter sitting on the coffee table, looking at her. "Are you feeling sick, Momma? You don't look well. Did you sleep here on the sofa? And where's Daddy? I wanted to show him the invitations, but now I can't find them. Do you want some orange juice? I served myself some, and a bowl of cereal. It's almost time to go to school. Are you going to be all right here by yourself? Momma? What is it?"

Marina told Violet that her daddy had been called back to the base late last night, and that she had been trying to wait up for him. And that she had ruined the invitations by spilling coffee on them. She promised that they would go buy more invitations that afternoon, and that Violet could take them to school the next day. Then she sent Violet on to school alone, though she usually walked at least part of the way with her. Violet still looked worried, so Marina gave her the best smile she could and said, "Go on, Sweetie. I just need to go and take a nice shower to feel like myself again." She watched until her daughter reached the corner, then took a quick shower, dressed and made a pot of coffee. She drank a cup, then another. She picked up one of Paul's cigarettes and lit it, though she hadn't smoked in years. She felt hollow, weepy, numb at the same time. Paul should be getting here any time now, she thought. Then what will we do?

Paul did not arrive until 10:30. He was freshly showered, clean-shaven. And he held himself in absolute control. "Paul…." Marina stammered.

He held up his hand. "Don't say a word. I want you to listen, and to listen carefully. If you agree to what I have to say, then we can go on. If you do not, or cannot, then there is nothing more to say, and we will get a divorce. There are no two ways to this; there is no middle ground. Understand?" Marina nodded.

"You betrayed me. You betrayed my trust and my love, by lying and by bringing that little girl into our lives. Now, I understand that back then, you were distraught and all, having just lost another baby. So, I guess it's understandable that you'd be desperate enough to want to adopt any baby at all. And it's obvious you knew how I'd feel about this one's bloodlines, so you didn't tell me. And then you went and put our names on the birth certificate, so to the whole world, this little girl is our own child." He seemed to shudder at the thought. Marina shook her head, but Paul put his hand up again, to quiet her.

"So the damage is done, and it is permanent. Damn it, Marina. The thing of it is, I love you. Even though you betrayed me, even though you've lied to me for eight years, I love you. I can't get around that. And I want to preserve this marriage. I will let you finish raising the little girl. But that's all. Don't expect me to be a daddy to her. I couldn't bear it.

"Now, I've thought about this all night, you understand. I've tried to convince myself that it doesn't matter that she's what she is. But I can't get around the fact that everything I've thought about her is a lie. And I know that blood will out. Marina, that little girl is gonna turn around and hurt you. Deeply. My daddy always said that those girls were cheap. She's gonna do something that you'll be ashamed of, and it's gonna happen, you mark my words.

"But, dammit, I also know that you love her. One of the things that attracted me to you was how you accepted and helped everyone, no matter what their background. That's who you are. So I will tolerate her. I'm not asking you to leave her. I know you can't.

Anything that has to do with her, you must take care of yourself. I don't even want to know about it. You buy her what she needs, clothes, school supplies, toys, whatever. I don't intend to be ungenerous. Just don't involve me, OK?

"And I don't intend to pay for her college, either. As far as I'm concerned, my responsibility ends when she finishes high school. After that, she is responsible for herself. Now it has seemed she's a smart girl, but I think that's just because you've been helping her. I don't think she'll ever make it to college. Anyway, it doesn't really matter to me.

"As for you and me, well, if you accept these terms, I want to continue being your husband. Things can't be exactly the same as before, of course. I mean, it will take some time, but I think I can come to trust you again. That's if you want. What do you say?"

Even though his words were harsh, Marina thought that perhaps, with time, he would learn to love his daughter again. Besides, there really was nothing that Marina could do. She'd never worked for a living; her parents had both passed away; she had a child to think of. And she did love Paul, no matter how hard this was right now. Her mother's words came back to her. If she didn't rock the boat now, it wouldn't sink. "I accept, Paul." Tears were threatening now. "I do love you, you know."

"I think I do know that. Oh, and Marina? What I said last night still stands. Don't ever tell her that she is adopted. I don't want her to know what her real background is. I swear, no matter how much I love you, I will leave. I could not stand to be a laughingstock in my own house."

"I'll never tell her, Paul. I promise." She drew close to him, and he put his arms around her. "One more thing. I'm going to be working on Saturday. From now on, I'll always be working on her birthday."

"All right." She looked around, then, "Would you like some coffee? I can make a fresh pot." He nodded, and she filled the coffeepot. "I can toast some bread, if you'd like." She looked at him. "I think we'll be all right."

After he left, Marina went to the drugstore and bought another pack of invitations. When Violet got home from school, she gave them to her daughter and told her to go ahead and write the information on them, then they could write the names on the envelopes together. Marina suggested she do that first, before doing her homework, and that she could do her homework after supper. Violet quickly agreed, but said that she didn't really have any homework that day, except to read two chapters of her library book, and she could do that before she went to bed. They finished early, and Marina suggested a light supper, since Paul would be working late again. In fact, he would be working late every day this week.

28

On Saturday morning, Violet woke up early and found her daddy in the kitchen, dressed for work. "Oh, Daddy! I thought you weren't going to work today. You're not going to be here for my party? I thought you wanted to see the clown! It's going to be a fun party, you know. I mean, all my best friends will be here, and we're going to laugh and sing along with the clown. And then all my friends are going to sing Happy Birthday to me, and I'm going to blow out all eight candles." She noticed that Paul had remained very serious, not at all playful like he usually was. "What's wrong, Daddy? Are you feeling sad because you have to work today? I understand."

Paul put down the newspaper, which had stayed in his hand throughout Violet's little speech. "You know what, Violet? You're growing up now. I think you're old enough to stop calling me 'Daddy.' I think you're old enough to call me Paul. That is my name, after all. Yes, I think eight is old enough to call your parents by their first names. You'll call us Paul and Marina from now on. Okay?" He gave her a smile with his lips, but his eyes remained serious.

Marina had walked in while Paul was talking. Paul looked at her with a warning in his eyes. "Don't you agree, Marina? Little Violet is growing up now, and so she should call us by our names." Violet looked from her father to her mother, a question in her eyes.

Marina hesitated for a millisecond. "Yes, Paul," she said, "If you say so."

"There! It's settled. Violet, you are not to call us 'mommy' and 'daddy' any more. It's Paul and Marina. Don't forget." He looked at his watch. "Oops! Time to get to work. Have a good day!" He whistled as he went to the car.

"Marina? Can't I ever call you 'Mommy' again?" Violet's eyes had filled with tears. "I don't think I'm going to like calling you by your name. None of my friends, not even the ones who are nine already, call their parents by their names. Do I have to call you Paul and Marina?"

Marina knelt down and swooped her daughter into her arms. "I'll tell you what, Sweetie, when we're alone, you can call me anything you want. But when Paul is here, let's do what he wants. After all, he is the man of the house, isn't he?" Marina would do anything not to see the pain in her daughter's eyes. "Now, I've got a lot of work to do, so you scoot on over to Nancy's house. Nancy's mom has a special surprise for you over there. Go on!" She watched as Violet made her way down the back yard and across the alley.

She turned on the oven and took out cake flour, eggs, milk, all the ingredients for a made-from-scratch cake that would end up looking just like the calico kitty that Cruz Romero was holding in her garage for Violet. Violet had been hinting about wanting a kitten for so long that when Marina had seen the calico at the pet store, she'd bought him on the spot. Then she'd asked Cruz to hold it until today. Of course, that had been before all hell broke loose. Marina tried not to think about that too much, because each time she did, she ended up crying. If only she hadn't told him! What had she been thinking! But it was too late now for self-recrimination. She was determined to do all in her power to make her daughter's life a happy one. She knew she could not protect Violet from her father's—from Paul's—indifference. But she could be there for her daughter, volunteer in her schools, take her places. By the time she finished frosting the cake, Marina had not only resigned herself to her new life, but had even managed to look forward to making all decisions about Violet without having to consult Paul.

Violet ran into the kitchen, letting the screen door slam behind her. "Mommy, Mommy! I love him! Oh, he's the prettiest kitty I've ever seen! Where did you find him, Mommy? Can I name him Nibbles? Oh, Mommy, I'm so happy. Look, he already knows his name." She put him down and walked to the door. "Here, Nibbles!" she called. The kitten meowed and ran to Violet. "See! He knows who he is, and that he's mine. Mommy, thank you! This is the very best present I could have wished for." She put one arm around Marina and hugged tightly, without ever letting go of Nibbles.

The birthday party was a rousing success. Jingo the Clown was funny, and entertained the girls with songs, balloons in animal shapes, and games that offered prizes to the winners. Somehow, each girl at the party managed to win a prize. He even managed to get Nibbles into the act, much to the delight of all the children, especially Violet. Marina served hot dogs and orange sodas, with potato chips on the side, then the cake, which was a huge success. The cat held four candles in each paw, and Violet managed to blow them all out in a single breath.

She wouldn't tell anyone what her wish had been, though. She said, "No, if I tell, then it won't come true, and I want this wish to come true."

Marina tried to get Violet to go to bed early, but she insisted on waiting up for her father. No matter how Marina tried, Violet would not be dissuaded. So when Paul walked in at eight-thirty that evening, Marina held her breath. Violet launched into her account of the party.

"Daddy, I wish you could have been here! Everybody had so much fun, and when Jingo the Clown was singing "Home on the Range," Nibbles thought it wasn't good at all, because he started meowing very loud. He didn't even let Jingo finish. But Jingo was really cool 'cause he turned it into a joke and we could all laugh with him. Then Nibbles just looked at us all and went over to sit by Mommy, just quiet and dignified as you please, like he was asking what all the fuss was about. You would have laughed as hard as we did. And then we played all these games with Jingo—did I thank you for hiring him yet? Mommy said it was your idea. Anyway, everybody won prizes and we were so happy. Oh Daddy, I'm sorry you had to work; it would have been wonderful if you'd been here. But look—I saved you a piece of cake." She took his hand and led him to the dining room, where she had placed a special plate for her daddy as soon as she heard the car enter the garage. Paul allowed himself to be led, but offered absolutely no expression while Violet talked.

When she had finished, he looked straight at her, with a coldness in his eyes that she had never seen before. "Violet, don't you remember what I told you this morning? Now, I don't want you to call me daddy anymore. My name is Paul, and that is what you will call me. Understand?" He paused until she nodded. Then he handed the plate to her. "And I don't want any cake. Take it back to the kitchen. And then go on to bed. It's late." Violet took the plate from his hand and walked slowly to the kitchen. Paul went into the living room and turned on the television set. He told Marina to sit there with him.

Violet went through the living room to the hallway that led to the bedrooms. She turned there, and looked at her parents as they watched some show on television. "Goodnight, Paul. Goodnight Marina," she said hoarsely.

Marina started to get up when Violet stood at the door, but Paul held her hand forcefully. "She really is old enough to take herself to bed, Marina." He raised his voice. "Goodnight, Violet. Go on to bed now."

She did not hear this last, for she had turned quickly and fled into the safety of her bedroom. Nibbles lay on the bed, asleep. She got into bed and turned off the lamp, holding Nibbles close to her face. "Goodnight Daddy, Goodnight Mommy," she whispered to no one. A sob caught in her throat. She tried to figure out what she had done to make her father so mad at her. She'd always been a good girl, or at least tried to be. When she'd made her First Communion and first confession last year, there hadn't really been much to confess. But maybe she just didn't realize what she had done. The priest said that sometimes that could happen to kids. They just didn't realize that what they did was wrong. But she just couldn't think of anything. Maybe—last week she'd been talking too much, and he had a headache. Maybe he just figured that she was so inconsiderate that he didn't want her calling him daddy. But no, that couldn't be it. She had apologized to him then, and he had said it was okay. He had even apologized to her too, for getting angry. No, that couldn't be it. Wait a minute. She had gotten that B in science on her report card. Science just wasn't her best subject. She had promised that she would raise that grade, but on Tuesday, she had gotten an 88 on her quiz. That must be it. He was disappointed in her. Well, she was going to change all that. She told Nibbles, "I'm going to work really hard in science class, Nibbles. Then I'll get good grades." She closed her eyes, finally giving in to sleep. "I'll make you love me again, Daddy. I'll be good for you," she added.

FIVE

From the door, the lady looked beautiful. Her hair was short and yellow and curly. She wore black high heels, a blue dress, and pearls around her neck and on her earlobes. Her eyes were blue like the sky and her lips were pink, like the carnations that grew in the yard. There were about thirty children in the room, all listening to their teacher, looking at her adoringly. The little girl stepped into the classroom and said, "Mees?"

The lady turned to her and said, "Mees? Mees! What's the matter, little girl, can't you speak English?" She turned to the other children, "Tell her what my name is, class."

The children replied in unison, "MISS SWANSON!!"

The woman turned again to the little girl, "Now you try it. It's your very first lesson. You can't come in if you don't say my name correctly! Why, we'd have to send you back to third grade...or maybe even first!"

The girl shrank back, shaking her head. She backed away from the door and from the classroom...the children were laughing, shouting, "MISS SWANSON! MISS SWANSON! Say it right or go away!" She covered her ears, but could still hear them. She wished she could just disappear, never have to go into that room.

29

October 1958

Toya woke up with tears in her eyes. The dream had been so real! Today would be her first day in fourth grade, and she was afraid. She was eleven years old, and she would be older than the other students. She would also be behind in everything, as she always was. Every year when her family returned to Harlingen from up north, she hoped against hope that her mother would forget to enroll her in school. Every year she was disappointed, and wound up in classes that she could not keep up with.

Her brother Beto was lucky. Because he had just turned 13, he could go to the special migrant school, where all the migrant secondary school students went. It didn't even matter that last year he'd been in fourth grade! Of course, he had to be in school from eight in the morning until five in the afternoon. And he would have two classes of everything, and never any time to color or play. But at least he would be with all his friends, and not with a bunch of strangers who would laugh every time he made a mistake.

Her mother called to her from the kitchen. "Toya! Get up and get dressed! You are going to be late to your first day of school. Hurry up now. Nana Yolita is going to braid your hair and then walk with you to the school."

Toya got up finally and quickly dressed herself. She liked it when Maria Dolores combed her hair, because she was so gentle that it never hurt. Maybe the day would not be so bad after all.

Maria Dolores came to the door and called out to her. "Aquí estoy, Maria Dolores, in the bedroom," she replied. "I have the rubber bands ready for my trensas."

Maria Dolores laughed as she saw her. Toya's hair was black and almost waist length. Every night, when she went to bed, she braided her own hair, or attempted to. The result in the morning was hair that was half-wavy, half-straight, and all messy. Taking up her brush, she started by expertly parting the little girl's hair, then brushing all the way through until the hair was perfectly smooth. It didn't take her long to braid the hair after that. Toya twirled and gave her a big hug, saying, "Yolita, I love you almost like a mother."

Maria Dolores responded with, "And you are a daughter to me! Now, come on. We don't want you to be late for school, do we?" They waved good-bye to Benita and went out the door.

Maria Dolores noticed that the closer they got to Lamar School, the slower Toya walked. She asked what the matter was, and Toya recounted her dream. Maria Dolores put her arm around Victoria and held her tightly for a few seconds. She explained that there are three kinds of dreams that people have. Some are memory dreams, in which we remember people or places we loved, or things we did. Others are message dreams, in which God is telling us something about our lives, or about our future. And still others are fear dreams, in which our own anxieties or fears take vivid shape. These last are sometimes called pesadillas, or nightmares, because they weigh heavily on our nights and sometimes on our waking hours. Also, sometimes they deceive us, because they masquerade as memory dreams or even as message dreams. One way to tell them apart, though, is that memory dreams and message dreams move us forward; they inspire us to act upon something in our lives in a positive way. But fear dreams hold us back; they make us shrink from doing something positive in our lives.

"What you have described to me, Toya, sounds like a fear dream. And we must defeat fear dreams by taking positive action. So, like my grandfather Diego always said, 'Ir adelante siempre.' Let's go forward with our heads held high. Here is the school; let's go into the office to register."

The school secretary directed them to the cafeteria, where tables were set up to register the migrant students who were returning from up north. Since Victoria had been a student there last year, it was an easy process to enter school. The lady who completed her registration said, "You're in 4-3, in room 25. Your teacher is, let's see, she's new this year, very pretty and very nice…yes, Miss Suarez. I'm sure you'll like her." Toya had a huge grin on her face. She couldn't believe she'd have a teacher mexicana!

She told Maria Dolores that she could find the room by herself, and ran on ahead, with her admission slip in her hand.

Maria Dolores walked to Margarita's house. She had not been to see her yet, as they had spent the last two days settling in again. But now she could help her friend for a few days, until she started working again in people's homes. It was still amazing to her, but she could always find work when they returned from up north. It would be maybe two weeks only, but at least for those two weeks, she could visit and help Margarita.

She felt a wave of nostalgia as she entered the old neighborhood. She wondered what Marina and Violeta could be doing now, or even where they were. Though it had been more than five years, it still hurt to think about them. Of course, as in all things, God's wisdom and love had led her to find Victoria, so the hurt was assuaged by the relationship with her other daughter.

30

Marina sat in the third row aisle seat in the school auditorium. Violet had the lead in the school safety play this year, and was doing really well. She had an enchanting way about her…but then, what else would her mother say? She wished Paul had seen his way clear to attend. But of course, that would have been impossible. Paul was always busy. That's just the way things were. When the play ended, there was a reception with punch and cookies at the entrance to the auditorium. Violet and Marina were talking to Nancy and her mother, making plans for a sleepover at Nancy's over the weekend.

Mr. Black, the school principal approached and asked to speak to Marina alone. Concerned, she asked him if there was a problem. "Oh, no, no, Mrs. Henderson. On the contrary. You see, KOB TV is starting a new campaign to encourage students to study science. Each week in November and December, they will be pairing a student from one of the elementary schools with a science professor from the University. It will be during their noon program. Violet has shown such an aptitude and interest in science and math that, well, we would like for her to represent our school." He smiled broadly. "Our turn is the week of November 15. She will be on with Dr. Evans, an anthropologist who specializes in the native cultures of the American Southwest. He's a fascinating man. Of course, we must have your permission to have Violet on the show. And, on the last day, we'd like to have you and your husband on also, if it's possible."

Marina stammered. "My husband and me? Oh, no, that would be impossible. I mean, I'm really glad that Violet has been selected for this, Mr. Black. But her father would be unable to come on the program. I could come on if you'd like, but her father…it would be impossible, you see." Mr. Black had a quizzical look on his face. "It's because of his job in the military."

Mr. Black broke out another of his famous grins. "Not to worry, Mrs. Henderson. If you'd like to come on the program alone, that would be perfectly all right with me."

Marina smiled at last. "Then yes, I'd be happy and proud to have my daughter on that television program. And I'm sure she'd be pleased too. May I tell her now?" Mr. Black nodded. Marina turned and called out to Violet, who was still talking to Nancy Romero. Violet came when her mother called. "Violet, I have some very good news for you. You're going to be on television, representing the school!"

"I'm going to be on television? Really, Mommy? Really, Mr. Black? Oh, how exciting! What am I going to do on television? Oh, Mommy, what'll I wear? Oh, I can hardly wait! Mr. Black, what am I going to do?" She knew that Mr. Black would be able to answer this question.

"Well, Violet. There's going to be a scientist on television with you. His name is Dr. Evans, and he studies ancient people and their culture, what their lives were like. He specializes in the people who lived here in New Mexico long before the white man came to America. Now, the format of the shows—you'll be going for a whole week—is that on Monday, Dr. Evans will explain what an anthropologist does and how he decided to become one. You'll be able to ask him questions…and I imagine that he'll ask you some questions about yourself too. Then on Tuesday, Wednesday, and Thursday, you will actually go to some places where he does his work, and maybe even help on a project. On Friday, you're back in the studio, and there will be a wrap-up, with final comments and observations from both Dr. Evans and you. How does that sound?"

"You want the truth, Mr. Black? It sounds a little scary, but also like a lot of fun. I do want to do it, oh yes; I do want to do it!" She looked over to where Nancy and her mother were standing. "Can I tell my friends about it? Please?"

"Go ahead! I'll give you more details as I get them." Mr. Black responded with a laugh. He turned to Marina. "She sure is a bundle of energy, isn't she? Mrs. Henderson, could you come into the office to sign the permission form? It's a requirement before I can allow Violet to actually go on television." They walked toward the office. "Mrs. Mercer, her teacher, will accompany her to the sessions. She will make sure that everything is done appropriately, so you needn't worry about your daughter at all."

Violet wanted to be the one to tell her father the news, and even though Marina tried to convince her daughter otherwise, she waited up for him to arrive from the base. "Paul? I have some news for you. It's really exciting; I think you'll be happy too. You know Mr. Black? He's the principal at my school? Well, today he asked if I would be on television. It's so neat. I'll be on television for a whole week, every day, for an hour a day. And that's not the best part. The very best part is that I'm going to meet a real scientist. I got chosen because I'm doing so well in science, you know?" She looked at Paul for a sign of encouragement. There was none. "And Dr. Evans he's, he's a anthra—anthra—Oh, I don't remember, but he studies people and their culture, and he's from the University, and he's real well known, and he's going to explain what his work is all about. And

I'm going to get to go to where he works and see for myself what he does. Oh, Paul, it's so exciting. Aren't you proud of me? I do hope you'll watch the program when I'm on…it'll be the week of November 15…." Violet grabbed his hand; he extricated it and looked at Marina then at Violet.

"So you're doing well in science, eh? Well, I guess Marina has really been working with you on that. Of course, anthropology isn't really a science, is it? I mean, there are no formulas or no math involved in it? But if you like it, I guess it's right for you. Anyway, I won't be here in November. Why don't you go outside and play? I need to talk to Marina in private." Violet dragged herself out the back door, but stayed close by.

He didn't even wait for her to leave. He said quietly, "I've received new orders. We're going to live in Japan for the next six years, at least. I'm leaving on Saturday. I'll find us a place to live, out in town, as you like, and then I'll send for you. You can come over the Christmas holidays. Unless you want to leave the kid here with someone and come with me now?" He looked away. "No, don't answer that. Tell you what. At least have her spend the night away on Friday, so you and I can have one last night alone together before I leave. And so she doesn't have to see me off on Saturday. Okay?" Marina nodded, but said nothing. She did not know how she'd explain this to her daughter.

Violet, standing at the back door, heard what Paul said to Marina. Tears blurred her vision before they spilled onto her cheeks. She had never figured out why her father hated her. She realized now that she probably never would. But there had to be some way, some way to regain his love. She still remembered how he used to play with her, back before her eighth birthday.

Well, at least her mother still loved her. The tears on her cheeks had dried. There was something she could do for her mother. She walked to Nancy's house, and spoke to Nancy's mother. "You see, since my father is leaving on Saturday, I thought it would be really nice if they could have an evening together, just the two of them. Could I spend the night here then?"

Cruz looked closely at Violet, smiled, and nodded. "Of course, Violet. Nancy wanted to ask you to spend the night anyway. I'm making hamburgers for supper. You want to eat here, or eat at home first?"

"I—I think I'd like to eat with Nancy, if that's all right. Mom and Dad can have like a date, you know?"

"Sure. Now go and tell your mother that I invited you to spend the night. She might not like it if she knew you asked me."

31

August 1963

Benita, Maria Dolores, and Toya walked into the church rectory in Pasco. Even though they had been coming to this area of Washington for six years now, coming into that parish office was intimidating. Benita spoke to the secretary. "We want make arrange for wedding. My daughter marry with Genaro Barrios. He no come this morning because he working, but he come in the night if necessary." This was the longest speech entirely in English that she had ever pronounced.

Mary Allen had been the parish secretary for eighteen years, and had seen it all in that time. She looked at Toya and walked to the pastor's office, closing the door behind her. "Father Zilligan, we got another one of those migrants trying for a quick wedding. The groom didn't even come in. The girl is about sixteen, and more than likely she's pregnant. She came in with her mother and another woman. Do you want me to send them away, or do you want to talk to them?"

"Now Mary, when have I ever had you send someone away? Send the girl in….alone." Father Zilligan watched his secretary walk back to her office. He knew she didn't like the migrant families coming in to the office, but after all, they were Catholics too, and he could not turn them away. Toya walked into his office. "Okay, young lady. I hear you want to get married?"

"Yes, Father," she replied. "Genaro and I got married by a judge last week. We eloped. But now we want the Church's blessing. Because it's not right to be living in sin." She did not look him in the face.

"Are you pregnant?" he asked. "Tell me the truth, now, girl. Are you expecting a baby?"

Tears sprang to her eyes. "Yes, Father, I am pregnant. The doctor at the clinic said the baby will be born in March."

Father Zilligan looked at her closely. "Heaven knows if I'm doing the right thing, girl. I should tell you to wait until you get home and get married over there." Toya started to say something. "No, no don't say anything. You'll be showing by then and it'll be much more difficult for you and for your child. We'll perform the convalidation tomorrow evening at seven. Don't be late, or I might change my mind! Now, go to Mrs. Allen and tell her you must fill out the papers. Do your section and tell your boyfriend to come to six o'clock Mass tonight so he can fill out his papers after Mass."

"Yes, thank you, Father! Genaro will be here tonight, and we will all be here tomorrow. Thank you, Father!" She took his hand and kissed it, like her mother had taught her to do. Then she hurried out and spoke to Mrs. Allen. Mary gave her the papers and then walked into Father's office.

"Father, maybe you should just round up all those couples out at the migrant camp and marry them. I'm sure there's more that need marrying out there." Her displeasure was making him impatient.

"Mary, no more of that, now. Do you hear? Now, go on out there, and make sure she fills out all the blanks correctly. Can you do that?" He motioned for her to leave.

The wedding was simple. Maria Dolores, Benita and Beto attended, as did Genaro's parents. After the ceremony, they bought fried chicken to take home so that both families could celebrate together.

At the end of August, Genaro's parents returned to Salinas, California. They made it a point to return in time for the start of school, so their children would not miss out. Since Beto, Jr. had been drafted on his eighteenth birthday, Victoria's father asked Genaro and Victoria to stay and finish out the season, letting Genaro do the part that would have been done by Betito. They traveled to Texas in late September. Genaro had finished eleventh grade in California that year, and though he could have attended school in Harlingen, he looked for and got a job at the canning plant there. Victoria stayed home; she should have entered ninth grade that fall, but chose not to.

When they got home, there was a bundle of letters from Beto Jr. He was in Vietnam, had been there since July. In the letters, Beto apologized for not telling them he was going over there, but he knew it would only make it hard for them "en los trabajos" if they knew. That was just like Beto, always thinking of others before himself.

32

Toya took it upon herself to write to her brother every other day. She had never liked writing in school; her English grades were always very poor. But she actually enjoyed chronicling the events in Los Vecinos for her brother. She always had some tale to tell about this neighbor or that one. Aurora la peleonera provided pages of fun, as did Gracie, the divorcee in 24, who had many "friends" drop by at odd hours. And of course, news of the family. His initial response to news of her marriage was less than enthusiastic, though he did remember Genaro from years past, and had no objection to him in particular. He just wished that Toya had waited, had stayed in school.

But, after scolding her in one letter, he congratulated her in the next, and wished her happiness with her husband. Toya was greatly relieved when she read that particular letter, which he wrote in the middle of November and she received at the beginning of December. In it, Beto also asked her, if she had a son, to name it after him. She thought this curious, and he must have too, for he added that he guessed being amid so much death, he thought he might like to have at least one boy named after him.

When she read that part of the letter to her family, they all grew very somber. Fear that Betito would be killed in Vietnam was always bubbling below the surface in the family. After a few minutes, Genaro broke the tension. "Boy! Am I glad he asked that! Toya wanted to name a son after me, and I didn't want to do that to any son of mine! Now, Roberto, that is a fine name. And he will have a middle name of Ruiz, too. That way there can be no doubt who he is named after. And if it's a girl? Well, we'll work on getting a Robertito as soon as possible!" Toya blushed furiously as both her parents laughed.

Five days later, on December 8, Toya finally had a chance to finish a letter to her brother. She had just sealed it and was going to place it in the mailbox out in front of the projects when she saw two men in uniform walking up the sidewalk that connected all the apartments. One of them carried a briefcase. Toya grew pale and dropped the letter on the table beside the door. They couldn't be coming here. Not here. She had seen this scene played out many times, with officers going to other homes. She stepped back from the door and prayed that they would pass by. Her heart was pounding, and the baby inside her kicked hard. Dear Lord, she thought, let it be somebody else. But who could she hope it would be? Mario, the seventeen year old from 321? Or Pascual Farias? She could not hope that either one of them. She peeked out through the screen door again. The officers consulted a paper, then approached her door.

"Pardon me, Ma'am. Is this the home of Roberto Ruiz? Roberto and Benita Ruiz?" She nodded. "Are they in, Ma'am? Could...could we come in, please?" Toya nodded and stepped back from the door so they could walk in, and she yelled out for her parents to come downstairs. She was crying already.

Beto ran down to find Toya and the officers just inside the door. The officers stood there awkwardly. Beto put his arms around his daughter. He looked at the officers, a question on his face. "My son is dead, no?"

Before they had a chance to answer, Benita came downstairs. She addressed her daughter. "Toyita, where are your manners? You have not offered these nice men anything." She turned to the officers. "Please, come into our salita and sit down." She took one by the hand and led him to the sofa. Would you like some coffee? I can make some right away. It is no trouble at all. You must have come very far. You look so tired. You know, my son, Betito, he wears a uniform like that sometimes. I have his picture right here." She turned to the end table and picked up her son's picture.

"Mami, ¿qué te pasa?" Toya asked quietly. "These men have to tell us something, Mama." She looked at her father, who motioned her to be quiet.

"Benita, Vieja, después hablamos tú y yo. Go ahead and make us some coffee." He watched as she went off to the kitchen, then turned to the officers. "You must excuse my wife, she takes time to hear bad news."

The older of the officers spoke. "That's understandable, sir. Mr. Ruiz, your son was a true hero who died in the service of his country. I'm sorry, Mr. Ruiz. I wish we had other news for you. Robert was a fine young man. He…"

The words sounded hollow even to himself. He looked down at his hands for a long time. When he looked up again, there were tears in his eyes. "I recruited Robert, Mr. Ruiz. He struck me as a good boy. He spoke well of his family, and wanted to help you. But I guess that now…uh, his company commander, uh—you'll be getting a letter from his company commander when his—when Robert arrives."

"When Robert arrives? When will that be?" Benita came into the living room carrying a tray laden with cups of coffee. She was crying now. "How long does it take?"

The officer looked at her, then replied, "It usually takes about five days after notification, Ma'am. Uh." He looked at Beto now. "Which funeral home should we contact about arrangements?"

Beto responded, "Garza. Please."

The officer nodded and stood up. "The funeral home people will contact you about your preferences. Of course, the Army has a funeral stipend." He shook hands with Beto. "If there's anything we can do, please let us know."

Toya spoke up then. "When—what day did he—did my brother die? Can you tell us that?"

He consulted his paper. "It was December 3rd, Ma'am."

Toya touched her stomach. "Betito Ruiz Barrios," she whispered. "¡Tienes que ser niño!" To the officers she said merely, "Thank you."

33

November 1963

Vi entered the house and took her shoes off at the door. Her mother was outside in the courtyard, tending her Japanese garden. Most Americans, if they took houses in the community here, tried to build American gardens. Not Marina. She asked the neighbors for help in restoring the garden to its Japanese glory. Since the last three tenants had been Americans, the garden had also reflected American styles. Marina, in her search to know the people and the culture, decided to use the garden as a point of reference and a way to make friends among the Japanese. It had worked well, and her Japanese garden was a source of pride and a perfect meditation garden. Vi opened the sliding doors that led into the garden and walked out. Water gurgled in the little stream as a crisp October wind filtered into the courtyard. She saw her mother at the end of the garden, engrossed in prayer. A cherry wood rosary hung from her hands. Her fingers unconsciously caressed the beads as she prayed. A single vertical line creased the area between her eyebrows. Even in prayer, that particular line of worry—of unhappiness?—never left her mother's face.

Vi knew that her mother had always tried to protect her from Paul's—when had she stopped thinking of him as "Daddy"?—coldness, but she hadn't been able to, not one hundred percent. Vi had become an excellent student, even to the point that she was graduating more than a year early. She had never made close friends in school, because she did not feel that she could invite them to her home. In the five years since they'd left New Mexico, Violet had changed from a talkative, expressive little girl to a reserved young lady. She only really came alive in class. Still, she managed to work well with others, and to do some community work as well.

She waited until her mother finished praying. "Mom," she began. "You know I'm eligible to graduate in December, if I choose."

"Yes, Dear, but I thought you'd decided to go another semester. I mean, as it is, you'll have just turned seventeen when you graduate, and…"

"But, Mom. I—I just got my acceptance letter from the University of New Mexico. And they offered me a scholarship too. I can start in January. Oh, Mom, please say it's okay!" She looked at her mother with eyes that begged her not to ask any questions, not to put up any obstacles. In truth, Paul had taken the letter to her at school, had given it to her as she left the school grounds. He had opened it, for some odd reason all his own; usually he didn't care if she was even alive. He told her it sounded like a wonderful offer, that she should take it, that it was time she got out on her own anyway, that it was for the best.

Marina took Violet into her arms. "Okay, Sweetie, okay. I give you my blessing. Oh, and I even have a surprise for you." She fished in her pocket and drew out something that she held tightly in her hand. "Do you remember the medallion your Nana Yolita put around your neck when she was taken away? It was round, with Our Lady of Guadalupe on one side and the Sacred Heart on the other?" She paused and Violet shook her

148

head. "Well, anyway, I was going through some old boxes, and I found it. Look!" She held up the gold chain and medallion and held them out to her daughter.

Vi reached out and took it. A flood of emotions ran through her. "I didn't even remember this. Oh, Mom, I wish she hadn't left us! Somehow I think many things would have been different." She looked more closely at the medallion. "Hmm…it's been what, about ten—eleven years? I wonder what she's doing? You know, I have this recurring nightmare, about when she left…the two men dressed all in green who took her away, she says goodbye, she is crying…and then, at the end, Paul shakes his head and says that it's for the best." Violet shivered involuntarily. Then, in a small voice, she added, "I always hate it when he says something is for the best."

Marina looked at her daughter. She wished she could heal the eight years of pain that Violet had suffered. But all she could do really was pray… "Here, Vi, let me put it on you. Then you can go ahead and tackle college at your age, tackle anything at your age, because you're under Our Blessed Mother's protection. Consider it a graduation gift from both Maria Dolores and me!"

34

March 1966

Victoria sat at her mother's bedside, humming the lullaby that her mother used to sing to her when she was a little girl. The cancer that had been consuming her mother slowly over the past year was now claiming her, and Victoria felt helpless. All she could do now was make her comfortable as possible, bathe her face gently with cool water when the fever raged, feed her clear broth when she could keep it down.

"Toya," her mother whispered. "Ya me está llamando el Señor. The Lord is calling me home. I have to tell you about your adoption."

"Shh, Mama," Victoria whispered in response. "Don't tire yourself out. I know the story; you told me when I was little. Don't you remember?"

"No, Mija," Benita was speaking again. "I told you the truth then, at least what I knew. But later I learned more. And I never told you. I thought I did the right thing. But now you need to know. Because I am going to die. And there is someone who loves you." She started coughing and could not continue speaking.

"Mama, just rest. Don't try to talk any more. Shh, now. Go to sleep. We'll talk later." Benita closed her eyes and drifted off. The younger woman waited for her mother to fall asleep. She looked around the bedroom, the death-room. There was a crucifix above the door lintel, and a picture of La Virgen de San Juan above her mother's bed. The cut-out wooden picture of her father made when he was in the service sat on the bureau. Beside it, a blue candle purchased at the church glowed, a testament to Benita's love for her husband, who had died two years ago in a freak accident in the fields. There was also a picture of Beto, Victoria's older brother. The last school picture of Juanito, who abandoned the family when he joined a commune last year, was next to Beto's. And finally, a little guardian angel statue representing Julio, the little brother who died when he was three months old, and who never got a chance to have a picture taken.

"So much suffering," Victoria thought, as she turned her attention to her mother once again. She wiped Benita's face with a washcloth, then walked out to the living room of the apartment they shared in the Los Vecinos housing project. She looked out the front door and saw Maria Dolores coming up with a platter of food. Then she looked at the clock that perched on the wall between the picture of John F. Kennedy and the print of the Virgin of Guadalupe. It was 11:30 already, and she had not even thought of cooking lunch. "God bless this woman," she thought. "I don't know what I'd do without her." Then she opened the door to let Maria Dolores in.

"Buenos días," Maria Dolores said brightly. "Good morning. How is Benita today? Is she feeling better? Here's this plate of food for you and your family. It's not much, just a little rice and beans, but it is prepared with love."

"Come in, Maria Dolores, and thank you. Mama is sleeping right now, but she is not well. She has a fever and is coughing a lot. She did not sleep all night. I'm afraid she is not going to last very long." Tears started rolling down her face. "She is suffering so much. I almost wish…" she crumpled down onto the sofa and covered her face with her hands. "Is it a sin to wish she could rest?"

Maria Dolores put the food on the table and put her arms around Victoria. She said nothing, but started humming one of the hymns from church. Victoria felt a sense of peace coming over her, and her sobbing subsided. She half-dozed in Maria Dolores's arms, almost forgetting her troubles.

There was a soft whistling wafting in the air, and Victoria straightened up. Genaro, her husband, was coming up the walk, with Betito walking beside him. Their son was two years old now, and the baby girl in Genaro's arms, Rosita, was eleven months old. Victoria got up from the sofa and went to the stove to heat up the food that Maria Dolores had brought. As she did so, a low moan came from the bedroom. She hesitated, then started to put down the food. Maria Dolores told her to attend to her family, that she would go in to see Benita. Victoria nodded and smiled gratefully.

Genaro took Victoria in his arms and held her for a moment. He could see what her mother's illness was doing to his wife and wished he could take away the pain. He also wished he didn't have to tell her he was leaving.

"I saw Tomás this morning, when I was going to the schoolyard with the children," he said. "They're leaving Saturday to Pasco. He says there's a job for me if I want to go with them. But I have to stay until the end of October."

"October? But that's more than six months, Genaro. What am I going to do for six months? How will I manage alone? Who will help me with the children when Mama gets worse?"

"I don't want to leave you here alone, but we need the money. I have been looking for a job since we came back last November. You know there is nothing here that will pay enough. I can send you money for the doctor or for…," he hesitated a bit, "…other expenses. I told him yes. He needed to know right away, so he could look for somebody else if I said no. We have lots of neighbors here at Los Vecinos. I'm sure they'll help you. I know that la prietita Chula—Maria Dolores—will help you out. She treats you like a daughter already. Look, Toya, I wouldn't go if I had a choice."

"I know, Genaro. It's just that all this is so hard." She leaned into him, seeking the support and strength she had so often found there. "I only hope God gives me the strength. Because I know I don't have it. Mira, maybe while you're there you can look for Juanito. I know it would make a difference to Mama if he would come see her." With those words, she gave her consent. She would have to face her mother's illness alone, face the fear of death and even death itself. She pulled herself together and finished putting lunch on the table.

In the bedroom, Maria Dolores was softly crooning a lullaby. Benita was half-asleep, but the song had made its way into her consciousness. She opened her eyes and looked at the mother of her only daughter. She tried to speak, but no sound came out. Maria Dolores shook her head slightly and spoke in her ancient tongue. Benita did not understand the words, but felt strangely soothed by them anyway. She felt the cool washcloth as it touched her forehead, her cheeks, her neck, her bosom. Soon…she would tell Victoria the truth soon.

35

Toya packed for Genaro's trip. Two pairs of blue jeans, six t-shirts for working in the fields, and two button shirts for going to mass, a pair of sneakers for work and his rubber sandals for when he went to the showers, and a pair of cutoff pants to put on after his shower. He had plenty of underwear, because even when he was not working, he would change in the afternoon. He would sweat so much that he said the clothes were uncomfortable if he didn't change. He was going to share living quarters with two single men, brothers, and they had already agreed what cooking utensils each would take. Genaro was taking a big pot.

They didn't have a phone in their apartment, but the Garcias who lived two doors down did, so they made an arrangement that Genaro would call person to person collect to himself when he arrived, and the family could then tell Toya that Genaro had arrived, without having to spend any money on the phone call.

Genaro started sending money right away. The first week, he sent a $200 money order, with a note asking her to reserve $50 "for emergencies." Thereafter, he sent $300 every week for ten weeks. In July, he skipped a week. Toya was frantic, because there was no way to reach him, and she was afraid he might be sick. But on the fourteenth of July, she received a long letter.

Toya waltzed into her mother's bedroom, carrying the letter from Genaro. "Mami, look! Genaro sent a money order for $800! When Maria Dolores comes this afternoon, I will go cash it at H.E.B. and buy groceries. I was getting tired of beans and rice, rice and beans." She bent down to give Benita a kiss. Benita was having one of her good days…in fact, had been doing well for three days now. The fever was gone, and she even seemed to be gaining a little weight. She started reading the letter. "Genaro says that he had so much work that he could not even go to town to buy a money order. The patron liked his work, and gave him more responsibility. Now he's going to be making $500 every week, until the end of October. I think things are going to be better now, Mami. And you are getting well, and…"

Benita interrupted Toya's gushing. "Mija, I am not going to get well. Yes, I feel better right now, but it is my time. I have to talk to you en serio." Toya started to protest, but Benita put a hand up. "No, Mija. You have not let me talk to you, and it is time. Diosito gave me these days of strength so that I can tell you. No me robes la intención. Now, sit down here." She patted the bed, and Toya sat down, subdued. Somewhere deep inside her, she feared what her mother was about to say.

"Toya, do you remember when Maria Dolores came into our lives?" Toya frowned a bit, as though trying to picture it. Benita continued. "Well, no matter. You were six years old then. She had called you 'Violeta' when she first saw you, because you looked so much like her Violetita."

"Ah, sí, Mami. I remember now. And she made migas for us, right, because we were moving in?" Toya cut in.

"That's right, Mija. Bueno, we did not know it at the time, but…ay no, I'm not telling it right. I wish she was here to tell you, pero she would not. I know. Mira, let me tell you her story from the beginning."

Benita continued with Maria Dolores's story. When she told her daughter that Maria Dolores had gone to Doña Chucha la partera, Toya surmised the rest.

"And I am that baby that Doña Chucha brought to you? Mami, are you telling me that Maria Dolores is my real mother? And that I was the result of a rape?" Toya's heart was beating very fast. Maria Dolores had never shown her anything but love, yet she was her mother and had given her away. It just did not make sense. "Did she give me away? Did she not want me? Why? Because she had bad memories of the rape? How did it happen? Why? Did she know when she came to live here?"

"Shh, calla, Hija. Let me finish the story. But first let me assure you that Maria Dolores did not give you away, that she wanted her baby very much. Escucha lo que pasó." When she finished the telling, Victoria just sat there, crying, saying nothing. Benita added, "Toya, fíjate bien que Maria Dolores could have claimed you as her daughter back then. She could have used Clemente as a witness, and the law would have been on her side. After all, we never adopted you through the courts. But she wanted only what was best for you. Imagine going through life hearing Rosita call another woman mother. Could you do it?"

"Mami, I'm not angry with either of you. I feel numb right now; I don't know how I feel, only that I am not angry. I just don't know how she did it all these years. How could she manage not to let it out? Maybe she was better off without her child? Is that it?"

"Toyita, Hija. Even before she realized you were her daughter, she looked at you with love. Remember how she would comb your hair for school?" Benita watched the different emotions cross her daughter's face. "Don't blame her, Mija. She wanted only what was best for you. And she thought is best that you not have a mother who could not give you a father."

Toya sat on the bed next to her mother. "Yes, it is hard to grow up without a father. People are cruel to children like that." She was crying now, but then she held herself still. "But I do wonder, though.... I wonder what happened to my twin."

"Pos...Yolihuani never heard from that family again. Y luego her friend Margarita Torres...they moved to Corpus Christi in 1958, because her husband was offered a job there. So even if they have sent her a letter in the last nine years, we would not know about it."

There was a gentle knock at the front door, followed by a creak as the screen door opened. "We're in here," Toya called out. They heard footsteps going into the kitchen, the water running, and more footsteps coming up the stairs. Maria Dolores appeared at the bedroom door, carrying a bouquet of flowers and a vase she picked up from the kitchen.

"Look, Mrs. Harrison got these flowers yesterday for the dinner, and she didn't want them no more, so she gave them to me. Aren't they pretty? I thought they would brighten up your room, Benita." She set the flowers down on Benita's dresser before she noticed the silence from the other women. She looked at them in the mirror, and saw they were watching her. She turned and spoke to Benita. "You told her." She came toward the bed and knelt in front of Toya. "Puedes perdonarme?"

Toya's tears flowed again. She touched Nana Yolihuani's hair, caressed her face. "What is there to forgive? That you were here, helping to raise me? That you allowed Mama to be a mother to me all these years? That you have loved me, and allowed me to love you?" Both of her mothers were crying with her now. She had not known how she would respond when Maria Dolores came, but her response was the most natural thing now.

"Nana Yolita, you have given me so much! I am proud to be your daughter, just as I am proud to be the daughter of Benita and Beto Ruiz!"

36

November 1966

The sun was bright but the wind was biting cold as Violet emerged from the student union building. She was on her way to her English class, the last of the day. Actually, after this semester, she'd be done with her basic requirements, and would be able to concentrate her energies on advanced anthro courses. Her hair whipped into her face, and she brushed it away, annoyed. One day soon, she'd cut it all off. Actually, the only reason she'd let it grow so long was because Paul had preferred it short. She snorted in frustration at herself. She'd been out of his house for almost two years now, not going back for holidays or any other vacations. Still, he had power over her.

She shook off the thought, and focused her mind on her work. Her full-ride scholarship didn't allow her to take a job during school time, but she always worked during vacations. Last summer, she had actually worked on a dig, as a gopher for a team of anthropologists who were piecing together the everyday life of a prehistoric Pueblo clan from the shards of pottery found at the site. It was very interesting, but she looked forward to next summer, when she would join Dr. Forrest in Central America, where he had contact with a group of Quechua Indians. They were going to observe rites of passage for both males and females in the tribe.

"Hey, I like the color that this cold brings to your cheeks, but if you stand out here any longer, you'll be missing English class!" Tom Jackson whispered in her ear. She elbowed him and stepped away.

"I didn't realize I was standing still," she said. "Oh, I guess I really need a break!" She smiled nervously. Tom always made her nervous. When he looked at her, he seemed to be looking into her. She covered her nerves by walking quickly toward the doors.

He kept pace with her. "The TA's gonna have us choose writing partners for this next assignment. You want to be my partner?"

She stopped and faced him. "Why? I mean, how do you know?"

He smiled enigmatically. "We Indians have our ways. Because I think you're interesting. You always have some sharp comments to make about the literature and the writing. I think we'd make a good team." He took her elbow and guided her to the door. "It's time to go in; the TA is fast approaching." He nodded down the hall at the teaching assistant. They walked in and took the last two seats available, three rows away from each other.

When class was dismissed, Violet left quickly, as usual. Tom caught up to her before she left the building. "Hey, what's the hurry? I almost had to run to catch you. Don't you think we ought to talk about the assignment, make plans?" He took hold of her elbow and guided her to the parking lot. "Come on, let's go eat. I know this little restaurant off campus where they serve the best tacos…you do like tacos, don't you?" He looked at her, and she merely nodded. "Good. Good, I'm glad. The restaurant owner is the mother of one of my best friends. She's Mexican, from Michoacan, I think. Or maybe from Veracruz. Anyway, she's a great cook, and it's not too expensive." He grinned. "I guess I've just destroyed the myth about the silent Indian, huh?"

She smiled at him. "Well...I never really believed that myth, anyway. There's too rich a history of storytelling among your people to believe that one." It was funny, but he had managed to relax her. She just wasn't nervous with him any more. She watched as he drove to the restaurant called "El Nopal". It was a small adobe building, decorated with desert murals on the outside, scenes of cacti and sagebrush backed by lonely mesas. Indoors, the scenes were of lush jungles and waterfalls with Mayan pyramids blended in.

The owner of the restaurant came out of the kitchen. "Tomás Jackson! Is good you come now. See the muro that Felix just finished." She pointed to the waterfall. "Is beautiful, no? Now looks like my tierra de Veracruz. Now my restaurant is just like me. Outside, puro New Mexico. Inside, puro Veracruz. Ni modo, is who I am." She laughed. "But why do I have you standing here? Vengan, sit down. You want to see the menu?" She led them to a small table near the kitchen.

"No, we don't need a menu this time, Doña Lili. Just bring two orders of tacos de picadillo. With a little bit of guacamole on the side." He smiled at the woman. "And some of your special hot sauce too."

Vi was entranced by Tom's deep, resonant voice. "You sound like a deejay," Violet said before she could stop herself.

"Well, actually, I was a deejay of sorts, in 'Nam," he replied.

"You were in Vietnam? When? For how long? Oh my gosh—how old are you anyway? I mean..."

His smile crinkled his eyes. "I know I look twenty, but I'm twenty-six. I did two tours in 'Nam, but I never went into the field because some general liked my voice and put me on the radio. I did see what the war did to my friends, though. It wasn't pretty. But that was half a world away and a lifetime ago. Now, tell me something about you."

"There's not much to tell, really. I'm an anthro major. I'm nineteen."

He looked shocked. "I finished high school early. And I'm mature for my age. I'm an Air Force brat. That's about it." She shrugged her shoulders and looked at him.

"Oh, I think there's more to you than that, Miss Henderson," he said. "And I'd like the chance to find it out. But not today. Today, we talk business. Now that we've got ourselves partnered for this assignment, where do we begin? Should we meet two more times? Three? Four? What do you say? Or should we just get married now? I'm all yours." He leaned over, twirled an imaginary mustache, and leered, and she burst out laughing.

She hadn't laughed like that in years.

37

August 1971

"Ju saw the letrero on da door en la eschool?" Maria Dolores insisted on speaking in English whenever she could. She had taken an ESL night class last year, and planned to continue her studies this school year.

"Cual sign, Nana?" Toya asked somewhat irritably. Her children, Betito, Rosa, and Genaro Jr. walked with them as they made their way home from Jefferson School. The baby, Maricruz was fussy as Betito pushed her carriage along the street. Toya knew the baby was hungry. Her breasts were full, and soon would start leaking. She didn't need her mother to be pushing her on anything right now.

"Da sign about da GED. So ju can finich high eschool. Ju chould go, Toya. Y Genaro too. No do it for self, do it for children. So ju can help dem wees homework. And so dey not be—como se dice avergonzados?"

"Embarrassed."

"Yes. And so dey not be embarrassed when you go to visit the school." Maria Dolores stopped walking and touched her daughter's shoulder.

"Why you tink I estudy Inglich? Because I like? Because is easy? Because my patrones want it? NO! Is because Genaro and Rosa want me see da books. And dey show me words pero I no know them. Pero ya I know more. And I can read. Con ellos."

They resumed their walking. Home was just two blocks away now. Toya wished Nana Yolita would stop pushing her, and told her as much. Maria Dolores apologized, then walked quietly for the rest of the way.

As they approached the house, Toya let out a sigh. "I wish my mother had lived to see this house," she said. "She always wanted to have a real house, where she could grow her own flowers and even vegetables."

"Jes," Nana Yolita replied. "And her own chilitos for her famous salsas. I mees her too, Toya. She gould be so proud of ju and Genaro. Ju stopped yendo to los trabajos, and Genaro got a year-round job primero at da canning plant, and now as janitor in the school. And you got out of Los Vecinos, and rent this nice house now. I know that Benita is looking from heaven and smiling."

They walked up the steps to the house. "And I have to feed Maricruz before she has a fit," Toya laughed as she took the baby into the bedroom. Her ill humor dissipated as she breast-fed her baby. Maria Dolores heard Toya begin to sing, "Una indita en Xochinacuas..."

The other children followed Maria Dolores to the kitchen, where she served them cookies and milk. While the children were eating their snack, Maria Dolores walked out to the back yard. "Que pasó, Lorito?" she asked her parrot.

"Ave Maria Purísima," intoned her parrot.

"Sin pecado concebida," Maria Dolores answered, laughing. She had taken great pains to teach that phrase to the parrot when she had bought him from a neighbor in January of 1969, a year after they'd moved to the house. The neighbor was frustrated because the parrot yelled out all kinds of insults as people passed by on the street. The woman had tried punishing the bird, hiding it, everything she could think of, but to no avail.

Finally, she had thought of killing the bird. When the neighbor mentioned that to Maria Dolores, she offered to buy the parrot instead. The deal was made quickly, and Nana Yolita found herself with a roommate that called out obscenities all day long.

Every morning, and each time she entered her room, Maria Dolores would greet the bird with, "Qué pasó, Lorito?" and the bird would retort with one of its varied curses. ""Vieja puta!" Or "Vete a la chingada." Or "Mira que cabrón!" Maria Dolores would then say "Ave María Purísima!" as she blessed herself. After about ten days, the bird replaced its normal response with "Ave María Purísima!" to which a delighted Maria Dolores replied, "Sin pecado concebida,"

The bird seemed to like this exchange, and repeated it each time. Maria Dolores had patiently taught the bird other Marian phrases. When she said, "Buenos días, Lorito," the parrot replied, "Buenos días, Paloma Blanca." Of course, over the nearly four years that they'd had the parrot, it learned other phrases, too, but all were things that would not embarrass the owners. When people passed by on the street now, the parrot would call out, "Buenos días le dé Dios" or "Ay, Nanita!" Or even, "Qué bonito periquito."

Genaro sneaked up behind Maria Dolores as she talked to the parrot. He grabbed her by the waist and swung her around. "Hey, prietita linda, if you talked like that to any man you met, you would win his heart! Toyita tells me that you are going to take another English class this year. Hmmm…I think maybe you have a boyfriend in those classes and that's why you are studying so much." He laughed as he said this.

"Muchacho! Put me down!" Maria Dolores swatted at his hands. "Stop all this talk about novios! I am much too old to be thinking of such things. I did not think of them when I was twenty; you think I will at forty?" She walked into the kitchen. Genaro followed.

"No, seriously, Nana. You are still a young woman. You could maybe find happiness still."

"Mira, Genaro. I am happy. Except for missing my Violetita. But to live with you and my Toya, and with my grandchildren. That is happiness to me. I was in love one time. And I married him. His name is Juan Lorenzo. And he waits for me in heaven. God decided that we should have only two months together, but our marriage was forever." Maria Dolores looked directly into Genaro's eyes, which was not something she ordinarily did. "Do you understand that?"

"Okay, okay! Don't get angry. I was just playing with you. Anyway, I don't know what we would do if you decided to leave us. So, tell me about this idea of yours that Toya told me about. You want us to go to school? Por qué? We are doing all right, don't you think?"

"Sí, Genaro. Is better than it jused to be. We do not go north to the camps any more. You have a good job that lasts all year. We do not have to get queso del gobierno. Pero let me tell you a little story so you can understand.

"Lass week, on Tuesday, I went to work for Mrs. Garza. Mrs. Garza, you know, finiched high eschool and even went al colegio for one year. Mr. Garza is an electrician, a good one. He estudied with another electrician, then got his license. He has own business. Dey have three children. The beeg son is in ten grade. Da girl, che is in eight, and the little boy is ten years old, he going to five grade. Ricky, da little one, he come in kitchen and ask for hot tortilla with butter. Mrs. Garza like me make tortillas, che save dem in hielera and use later. I tell him jes, and he sit. He have new cuaderno, and he put name on. I ask him what is, and he say is for eschool. He is happy estart eschool again, because he see friends and because he learn new tings. He tell me he wants to be scientist when grow up. He say brother Mark be electrico engineer, but he, Ricky Garza estudy insectos in collich and become ento-, I cannot say word. I ask what is collich he talk about, an he tell me is where he go when he finich high eschool. He no say **if,** he say **when**.

"Okay. So I tink when I talk to Betito. Betito no want to talk eschool estart. He like better no go to eschool. He say if he finich eschool, maybe he get good yob. He say if he leave eschool antes, maybe he get a good yob sooner."

Genaro was shaken by Maria Dolores's story. He never thought his son would want to drop out of school. He certainly did not want that for his son. He knew that his and Victoria's life would have been much better if they had finished school. The Mrs. Garza that Maria Dolores was talking about, her youngest sister, Patty, had been a year ahead of Toya in school. But she had finished high school and even gone to college. Now she was going to be a teacher at Lamar, the school where he was a janitor. And she was making more money in her first year as teacher than he made after three years as janitor.

"Ju see, Genaro, why want ju y Toya estudy? Ju see is importante children see ju learn? Maybe, they want learn more too. Maybe they have better life."

"I think, Nana Yolita," Genaro said, "that you are a very smart woman. I think that you are showing us the way for us to have a better family. Toya and I will both study, with your help. You will have to study too. And that way, our children can study with us. And we can all do homework together. I can see it now. We will have to get a bigger kitchen table, so we can all put our books on it! Ah, que mi Prietita Chula, you are making us all do what your grandfather said, no? 'Go forward always, never go back.' We know that saying by heart."

Maria Dolores rapped him on the head. "Si live saying with hearts and heads, da children have better lives. Is what important, no?"

38

March 1972

Violet reached into her mailbox at the student union and retrieved two envelopes: a pink one in her mother's familiar handwriting, and a white one from the University of Toronto. She hugged the latter to her chest and breathed a prayer. "Please, God, let it be good news." Rather than open it there, in front of everybody, she stuck it in her bag and ran out to her bike. She pedaled quickly; and soon she was in her living room, envelopes in hand.

She put her mother's letter aside and tore the end off the other one. The letter slid out easily. It read,

March 19, 1972

Dear Miss Jackson,

It is with distinct pleasure that I inform you that you have been accepted as a teaching fellow in our Ph.D. in Anthropology Program.

This 3-year Fellowship allows for the cost of your tuition and includes a stipend for living expenses. In return, you will be expected to teach three sections of the introductory course in the fall and spring semesters.

I have asked to serve as your advisor during your tenure here. In speaking with Dr. Bell at the University of New Mexico, I find that your interests and mine most certainly mesh, and I believe that we shall be able to help each other in our endeavours.

I do trust that you will be available to begin in July, as I would like you to join me in the field in Vancouver. I have a project with a Native American tribe there and would most certainly enjoy your help on it.

Please call me directly should you have any questions.

Sincerely,
Alain P. Bouchard
Alain P. Bouchard, Ph.D.
Professor of Anthropology
University of Toronto

P.S. I look forward to working with you.

Vi was ecstatic. She called Dr. Bell's office, but he was not in. She left a message that mystified the secretary. "Just tell him, 'Thank you!' He'll understand." She would see him in class tomorrow anyway.

She stood to go into the bedroom, and the pink envelope fell to the floor. Guiltily, she picked it up. She had forgotten her mother's letter. Well, no harm done, really. She opened it and began to read. Marina informed her that Paul was retiring (finally) and that they had decided to settle in New Jersey, about an hour from New York City. Marina still had some cousins living in the area, and she wanted to renew their relationship. Paul had no living relatives, so he did not really mind where they lived.

Marina did not expect a reply to this letter, as they would have moved by the time Vi could write, so she would write again as soon as they were settled. Perhaps Violet could find a way to come visit. She would love to meet Vi's husband. "Boy, wouldn't Paul like that," she thought. Then she laughed to herself. She could just imagine Paul's reaction to Tom.

She looked at the clock. Tom would be home soon. They'd planned a special night out, in celebration of their first anniversary. They had gotten married in a small civil ceremony. Felix was best man, and his mother Lydia, better known as Doña Lili, her matron of honor. Afterward they'd gone to Doña Lili's restaurant for dinner; Doña Lili surprised them with Mariachi music and a huge wedding cake. All the patrons got complimentary wedding cake for dessert, and all joined them in a wedding waltz. Doña Lili had taken the top layer and stored it in the restaurant's deep freeze. She told them, "Is for good luck. In one year, you come and we celebrate your anniversary. We eat all wedding cake then." Tonight was the night.

Violet thought it best to save her news until after the dinner. She decided to wear Tom's favorite dress, a black sheath with scoop neckline that showed off the pendant he had designed for her. "I name you Bold Deer," he'd said when he first put it on her. "You are bold in your studies and your curiosity, but timid as a deer when you are asked to reveal yourself to others." It had not been a reproach, but a description. Tom never reproached her for who she was. It was this total acceptance of her that had finally melted her resolve and caused her to say yes the fourth time he asked her to marry him.

Doña Lili outdid herself on the dinner. "No menus for you tonight. As your madrina, I have arranged everything." They started out with a salad of tender hearts of palm with slices of avocado and julienne jícama on a bed of bib lettuce. Then Chicken Breast Adobado with saffron rice and steamed crookneck squash, peas in the pod, and baby corn, with cauliflower florets. Dessert was, of course, wedding cake with a lemon sherbet that Doña Lili herself had made.

Felix and his mother joined them for dessert. "So, how's it feel to be an old married man?" Felix teased Tom. "I bet your florecita here keeps you on your toes!" Ever since he'd learned Vi's given name, he called her the little flower.

Tom laughed with his friend. "Truly, she does. You know, she turned in her Master's thesis nearly two months early, and still it received an award. Even though the graduation is in May, she's all done at school and could be lazy if she wanted, but already she has started on a project that interests her. Why don't you tell them about it, Vi?"

By this time, Violet was blushing. "Well, I—I just got curious to identify the commonalities in the rituals and mythologies of the various Native American tribes and nations. I mean, anthropologists have studied the individual tribes, and archaeologists have too, but I haven't seen an extensive, broad-based study of the common strands among them. I would perhaps like to see if—oh, I don't know exactly. If different migrations into what became the Americas originated from the same source, or.... I just don't have it fully defined in my own mind yet, but I'm working on it." She looked around helplessly.

Felix and Doña Lili just looked at her. Felix let out a soft whistle. "You're looking at a lifetime of work there, Vi. But I'll sure be interested in your findings, since I descend not only from the Navajo, but also from the Maya, thanks to Mami here. You will keep us posted, won't you?" Vi nodded her agreement.

Vi entered the apartment first and went straight to her desk, where she retrieved the letter from Dr. Bouchard. "I got some really good news today," she said, extending the letter to Tom. She continued as he read. "Working with Dr. Bouchard on his project will advance my own project so much! Oh, Tom, it's like this offer was made to order for me! GW accepted me also, but their offer doesn't hold a candle to this one! I'm so excited!" She stopped, noticing the expression on his face. "What's the matter, Tom? What's wrong?"

"Nothing much," he replied. "I also got an acceptance letter today. I'll start training at Quantico in July." He opened his arms wide and she stepped into them. He enfolded her in a deep embrace. "You know what? It's probably a good thing you're going to be so busy in Canada. An agent told me this afternoon that he hoped my wife had an interesting hobby, 'cause training takes up most of a novice agent's time anyway. At least we've got—what?—two and a half months before we separate. We can go up to Toronto and find suitable housing for you, and we can generally vacation for a while. How does that sound to you?"

"It sounds wonderful. God, I'm so fortunate to have you as my husband! Any other man…"

"Any other man would not be your husband," he interjected. "Now, stop talking and come here, wife. We have an anniversary to celebrate."

The next morning he fixed her breakfast. He was still a better cook than she was. As they ate, she told him about her mother's letter. He smiled brightly, "Hey! So I'll finally get to meet your family. I know you have issues with your father, but since he's retired, he should be able to make your graduation. And your mother—I mean, you don't talk much about her, but I know you love her very much."

"Oh, yeah? How do you know that?" she challenged.

"By the way you always wear that medallion she gave you. I know you don't do it for religious purposes. So it must be because it belonged to your mother."

"Well, actually—though my mother did give it to me before I left Japan—it was actually a gift from my nanny. She gave it to me when I was six, when she went away. But I guess Mom had put it away for me, or something." She frowned. She had a fleeting memory of an argument between her parents, her father demanding that the medallion be thrown out. She looked at her husband, "Anyway, she thought it important that I have it when I left her. I've worn it ever since." She looked at him and half shrugged. Then, feigning indignation, "And what do you mean, you know it's not for religious purposes!"

He raised his hands in front of him, as if to protect himself. "Nothing! I mean nothing," he replied. "But you are going to invite your parents to the graduation, aren't you?"

"Yes, of course, as soon as I get their new address," she demurred.

"Oh, by the way, you haven't ordered your graduation announcements yet, have you?" he asked.

"Uh—no," she replied. "Why?"

"I'm going by the university bookstore today to order mine. I'll order some for you, too. How many do you want? And, how do you want your name written?"

"Jackson. Violet Jackson. As to how many, I don't know. What's the smallest number we can order? Ten? Twenty-five?"

"I think it's twenty-five. OK, then, that's how many I'll order. Uh, I hate to leave you with the dishes, but I have an appointment with my faculty advisor. You know, final details and all."

"Go ahead, Tom. I'll wash them. It's only fair, anyway. Listen, do you think it would be a good idea to have a little party after the graduation? I could ask to use the community room by the pool. It doesn't have to be much, just some snacks and a cake. Maybe a pool party? What do you think? It would give Doña Lili a rest too…you know, she's always cooking for us, maybe this time she could just come and enjoy herself."

Tom smiled at her once more. "That's a great idea, Darling. Why don't you do just that? I bet my sisters would be glad to help us with sandwiches and snacks. I'll give them a call later. See you at noon?"

"Yes…at Doña Lili's. Felix said last night that he had something to show us, remember?"

He nodded as he walked out the door.

Violet cleaned the kitchen, then went and dressed in her favorite outfit: khaki shorts and blue tank over white tee. She pulled her hair to the front over her right shoulder and braided it. She had not cut it since arriving in New Mexico, and it was now at her waist. Tom loved to brush it, and she loved him to do so.

The community room was available, as was the pool, so she reserved both, then went to the party store to buy decorations for that day.

She arrived at the restaurant at 11:30, and showed Doña Lili what she had bought. The older woman seemed a bit miffed at first, because the party would not be at the restaurant, but Vi teased her out of it by talking about the pool party and how much fun it would be, that Doña Lili could wear her bikini and attract a nice-looking man. Her friend finally laughed and said that she would provide the cake, if that was OK by Vi and Tom. Vi agreed.

By the time Tom arrived, Felix had joined them and was fully participating in the conversation. He asked them both to go to the studio he had just built behind the restaurant. With a wink to his mother, he said he had a surprise for them. "Go on," Doña Lili said to them. "By the time you return, your food will be on the table. Vayan. Les va a gustar. I'm sure you will like his surprise."

This was the first time Violet had been in his studio. Actually, it was two rooms, the first a sort of gallery, and the second room was where he actually painted. This way, people could view his finished work without "accidentally" uncovering a work-in-progress. The gallery was sparsely furnished, just a couple of chairs and a bench, with three small tables of varying heights. Even these had been built by Felix, and seemed artwork on their own, painted in bright pastels.

The walls were ecru, with boxes that acted as shelves attached to them at different levels. The boxes echoed the bright pastels of the furniture. On these shelves were Felix's paintings: several landscapes of New

Mexico, in hushed pastel tones, as well as landscapes of Mexican jungle in rich jewel tones. "Yes, that's Veracruz," he said in response to Vi's look. "I visited there with Mom two years ago, and I can't seem to get it out of my mind. It's such a contrast to New Mexico, and yet they seem to complement each other."

"You know, they do," she agreed. "But I'm most fascinated with your portraits, Felix. I never knew you did portraits too. This old woman, for example," she said as she approached the painting. "I know she's a regular at the restaurant. I've seen her there many times. And this portrait doesn't look EXACTLY like her—I mean, that's not what you were trying to do, is it? But you have captured her essence. It's amazing!" She studied the portrait for a few seconds. "And this background! I don't think I've seen a landscape as a background to a portrait before, not like this, anyway. Why mountains?"

"Carmelina Sáenz is from Saltillo, Mexico. Mountains are her natural backdrop," he replied. He shrugged, then moved toward the door between the rooms. His eyes seemed to dance. "Would you like to see my studio now?"

He opened the door to the other room and let them enter first. In the center, mounted on a tripod, was a portrait of Vi and Tom together. They both gasped as they saw it. The background shifted from mesas and pastels on the left to a mountain with a river meandering down towards a city on the right. The transition was so well done that it looked possible. Tom and Violet were next to each other, he on her left and slightly behind, with his right arm around her shoulder. She was leaning back on his shoulder, her right hand holding his left hand. Tom exuded strength, confidence, and gentleness at the same time. Violet seemed relaxed and happy next to Tom, but somehow there was a tension also, as if she were waiting for something bad to happen.

Felix broke the silence. "I hope you like it," he said, "because it's your graduation present, and your wedding present too—I never gave you guys anything last year."

"Felix, it's just, just unbelievable," Vi responded with a hug and a kiss on his cheek. "I'm deeply touched by your insight. I think you've captured both of us really well."

"So do I. My friend, I am honored by your gift." Tom embraced his friend. "We will treasure it always."

Violet looked at the portrait again. "But I have one question about it. Why did you give me a mountain as my backdrop? I mean, I was born in deep south Texas, where the highest ground, according to my mother, is the freeway overpass. My father Paul is from Ohio and my mother originally from Germany. But you didn't know that, did you?"

"Actually, no, I didn't know that. And the entire background was going to be a mesa, but somehow the mountain seemed right for you. I don't know. Call it artistic license." Felix laughed and shrugged.

The three friends were standing together, arms around each other when Doña Sofía appeared at the door. "Is time to come eat, supper is served," she said. "Bring the portrait. We can show off before you take home with you." The four went to the restaurant and had their supper together.

By the time the invitations arrived, Tom had the new address for the Hendersons. He mailed out the invitation himself, with a note to Vi's parents. He included a picture of the portrait that Felix had made of them, "so you won't be meeting a stranger," he wrote.

Marina's response was addressed to her daughter. She would be delighted to attend the graduation and the party afterward. Could she come and spend a week with them, if that was not too much to ask? She would, of course, take a room at a local hotel, if Vi would make the reservation for her. Paul would not be able to attend. He was looking at some investment opportunities, and that particular weekend would be a busy one for him. He did, however, extend his congratulations to both of them.

When she received her mother's letter, Vi decided to call her. Paul answered the phone. "Paul?" She hesitated before continuing. "It—it's Violet. How are you?"

"Well, I'm fine, little girl." Coming from him, "little girl" sounded like an epithet. "I imagine you want to talk to Marina. Let me get her."

"Wait! I—well, I've done it, Paul. I have a Master of Science degree in Anthropology. And I was offered a fellowship to get my doctorate at..."

"Anthropology, huh. Well, now, that's not really a science, is it?" Vi could almost see him hitching up his pants. "I guess you couldn't make it in chemistry or something real like that." He snorted into the phone. "I see Marina coming down the hall. Here she is." He handed the phone to his wife and mumbled something about Violet.

"Hello? Violet? Vi, is that you, Sweetie? Oh, I've so longed to hear your voice!" Marina half-sobbed into the phone. "I was thrilled to get your invitation. And that picture of you and Tom! Oh, my dearest, I'm so happy for you. He seems like a good man," she was really crying now. "I've prayed so much for your happiness."

"Mom, he is a good man. And you will get to know him when you come for graduation. But you're not staying in any hotel. We have an extra bedroom in our apartment. Actually, we've used it as a study. But there is a bed in it, and we would love for you to stay with us. Please say that you will!"

Marina arrived three days before the graduation. Vi fell into her arms as soon as she saw her at the airport. Though Marina had called Vi regularly, it had been six years since they'd been together. They both felt the distance melt away as they held each other.

Tom stood by while the two women embraced, watching. He had thought that he would find a resemblance between mother and daughter once he saw them together, but except for the fact that both were fair complexioned, he could not find it. Even Marina's dark brown hair was a far cry from Violet's blue-black hue. Well, perhaps she looked more like her father. He would probably never know, because Vi never talked about him. She had warned him off that subject early in their relationship. He figured the man had been unfaithful to her mother, and Vi had probably caught him in the act or something.

The two women spent most of their time together preparing for the party. Tom's sisters were making sandwiches, and Doña Lili was contributing a cake, but Marina had some old family recipes for fruit and nut snacks that she had brought along, and mother and daughter prepared them together. Tom came into the kitchen to taste their creations, especially since Vi had made something from scratch. Cooking had never been her strong suit; this was a side of her that he had never experienced. It was nice to see the two of them working together like this.

After graduation and its attendant celebration, they had another week to spend together. Tom joined in as they rode and walked around familiar places, places Marina remembered from her stay there so many years before. Marina told Tom stories of Vi's childhood that he had never heard, and he shared his life story with them. His sisters had raised him, because his mother died when he was but four years old. His father had always been there for them, but remarried when Tom was fourteen. Tom had elected to stay with his sisters when his father and the new wife moved to Texas.

His sisters always remarked about Tom's frequent need for solitude, to renew his spirit. They often told Vi that it was a blessing for him to have a wife who was dedicated to her work, because most other women would demand a lot more presence from Tom. Tom shared with Marina his need for what he called "independent dependence" because of losing his mother at so young an age, and then his father to life's circumstances.

Vi knew all this, but he exhibited such vulnerability when he shared the story with Marina that it made her love him even more. And Marina's total acceptance of Tom, of who he was, made Vi love her more also. It was with great difficulty that she said good-bye to her mother on Saturday.

"Maybe you can come to Newark before you go on to Toronto," Marina said to them as they waited for her plane to board. "I would really love to have both of you there."

"And maybe Paul will have some investment opportunities to look into or something," Vi responded, then immediately wished she had not said it.

Marina lowered her eyes. "I—yes, I guess Paul would probably have to be gone when you visited." She looked up, into Violet's eyes. "He does have his good qualities, you know. And we're married in the Church."

Vi swallowed hard, then replied, "I'm sorry, Mom. Tom and I will see about that visit, won't we, Tom?"

"Yes. I think we can arrange it. I am planning to go with Vi to help her find housing, etcetera before I go on to Quantico. We should be able to get to Newark on the way there." Tom felt a little out of the loop. They had not discussed Paul during this visit. He imagined it was because Vi did not get along with him, but this comment went further than that. It didn't seem to be about infidelity. He couldn't figure out what it was all about, but was not too worried, though. He knew that in time, Violet would confide in him, just as he always wound up confiding in her. It had been that way since they first met.

The final boarding call was made, and Marina took off. Vi and Tom turned to leave the airport. "I'm sorry if I made you uncomfortable back there," she said. "I guess you can tell by now that Paul and I don't get along very well." She looked into his eyes. "But I can't really talk about it yet. Maybe someday."

Tom held her close. "Don't worry, Bold Deer. I will be ready to listen when you are ready to talk. Don't I love you more than anyone else on earth? Now come on, let's go to the gallery. I told Felix we'd help him set up for his showing tonight."

She groaned at him, pretending not to like the idea of setting up the gallery. Actually, she was fascinated by Felix's art. He did wonderful landscapes and still lifes, infusing them with light and color combinations that seemed natural yet almost surreal. But his portraits were extraordinary, capturing the essence of the subject to a degree that was uncanny.

The night after her mother left, Vi had a nightmare. Paul was in a coffin, but held his hands out so that she could not approach to pay her last respects. She woke up in a sweat, and told Tom her dream. He told her she was just reacting to Paul's decision not to attend her graduation.

39

Three days later they received a call from Marina. Paul was dead. He died of a heart attack, while Marina was cooking supper for him. He didn't call out or fall or anything like that. He had been watching television, sitting in his favorite chair. When she came to call him to supper, she found him passed out, which was odd for him, because he never slept in the afternoon. She checked him immediately and then called the ambulance. But it was really too late, for Paul had been dead already.

Tom could not believe his ears when Vi said she would not go to the funeral. "Violet, I know you and your father have been estranged. That's why it is important that you pay your last respects to him. Be reconciled, at least symbolically. We'd just have to alter our plans a little bit, go there before we go to Toronto."

But Vi was adamant, even when he offered to go with her. She shook her head and started sobbing. "I lost my father when I was eight years old. He died then, and I mourned him for too many years to mourn for the man that just died."

She finally told him what had happened so many years ago, not far from where they lived now. "I—he thought I failed at something. In his eyes, I was no longer worthy of his love, Tom. All of a sudden, he didn't want to be my daddy anymore. All of a sudden, I had to call him Paul. Oh, he was polite to me, and I never lacked for anything. But I had no daddy. And nothing I ever did fixed that. When we went to Japan, I became the perfect student there. I even graduated early, because I took extra classes, all to please him.

"But when I was offered the scholarship to the University here, he said I should take it, I should leave home right away, and—and not to bother to come home for holidays." She cried as if she had never cried before. Tom hugged her close and swore under his breath. Now Tom understood her much better, understood why she found it so hard to trust and even to love. He swore then that he would do everything in his power to help her overcome the pain that ruled over her life. No matter what changes there were in her life, he would never abandon her, never withdraw his love and support from her.

40

June 1980

Maria Dolores looked around the Brownsville Hannah High School gym as she waited for the ceremonies to begin. She looked up to the stands and located her family. They all waved at her: Victoria, resplendent in her maternity dress—pregnant again after nine years. Genaro, in business attire. Roberto, still called Betito, at sixteen very handsome and resembling his namesake. Rosa had just celebrated her quinceañera. Genaro Jr. would enter ninth grade in September, and Maricruz, truly a handful at nine, was hopping up and down, waving both arms at her grandmother.

What changes there had been! Genaro had completed his GED within four months of starting, then worked nights at school and attended classes at TSTC. Within two years he had opened his own business, a janitorial service he called CMC: Cleaning Maintenance Company. The business cards also read "We clean your place of business Con Mucho Cuidado." The business had grown to include seventeen employees.

Genaro himself went out on jobs only once in a while now, to spot-check his employees' work.

Toya took nine months to finish her GED ("And I FEEL like I've had a baby!" she'd quipped.) and became a teacher's aide at Jefferson School. Then, at her teacher's urging, she enrolled in college in Brownsville. It took her six years to graduate, taking 18 hours each summer and 9 each regular semester. Her principal had been a big help, letting her work after hours in the office to make up for the time she spent student teaching. She became a teacher two years ago. Now she was planning to get her administrator's certificate. It seems that once she started, she could not stop going to school!

Maria Dolores thought of her other daughter, Violet. She wondered how she was doing, if she was happy. She prayed for her every day, and for Marina too. She knew that Cihuapili had them covered with her manto. They must both be under Our Lady of Guadalupe's protection.

The meeting was called to order, and Maria Dolores's attention snapped back to the stage. The school principal welcomed everybody to Hannah High School, then asked the JROTC to present colors. The senior class president led the pledge of allegiance. The principal passed the podium to the judge. Judge Valdez thanked her, then introduced the two guest speakers, who told their inspiring stories of hard work leading to personal success. One spoke in English, and the other spoke in Spanish.

Then the judge himself spoke to the people who were about to take the oath of citizenship. "Of all the duties and responsibilities that I, as a federal judge, must perform, this one in particular gives me great joy and pride," he began. "My own father was a naturalized citizen, and he never failed to impart to me and my brothers how important it was to be proud of this great country of ours. In these United States of America, it does not matter what our cultural heritage is, or where we were born, or where our parents were born. We can all be proud of our origins, and still be proud Americans. I am going to call out the countries of origin, and I would like please for you to stand up when I call out your birthplace, and remain standing for the oath of office. Mexico. Yes, there are two hundred thirty-two of you. Nicaragua. Twenty-five. Ghana. Ten. Venezuela. Seven. Nigeria. Six. Vietnam Five. Germany. One. Italy. One. And Romania. One. That is a total of two hundred eighty-eight of you who will, in a few moments, become citizens of the United States of America. You have each of you studied for this moment, practiced for this moment, anticipated this moment for many months, some of you for many years. I ask you now to raise your right hand and repeat after me, stating your own name after the I. Let us begin. I, _____, do solemnly swear...."

Maria Dolores was swept up in the emotion of the oath of citizenship. She found herself crying, even though she and Toya had practiced over and over. She had come such a long way! "Grandfather Diego, *Teoxihuitl*," she half-whispered, "*mire nomás hasta donde he llegado.* Look how far I have come. You told me to go forward always, never back. You are here with me, as is the Lady. Thank you, Cihuapili, for your guidance." She pictured them as she had seen them in her dreams. She imagined that they were both smiling down at her, approving of what she had become. At fifty, she was nearly twenty years older than her parents had been when they had died, and nearly as old as her grandfather's age at his death. She was taken out of her reverie when her name was called out.

Betito was close by, camera in hand. "Nana, over here!" She turned and he snapped her picture. "Come on, they're giving you your citizenship papers. Come up here and the judge will give it to you!" She followed him and got up on the stage when her name was called. Betito took a picture of her with the judge. Then she walked across the stage and down the other side. Her family was waiting for her at the exit. Genaro picked her up and twirled her around. "I guess we should call you

'Grandma' now that you're an Americana," he teased. "This is an occasion to celebrate! Where shall we go for lunch?"

"McDonald's!" Maricruz piped in.

"No way, Shortie!" replied her older brother. This is a special occasion. I say we go to Matamoros for lunch! How about Los Portales?"

"How about Blackbeard's, on the Island?" ventured Rosa. "I've never been there, but they say it's good."

"Yeah," piped in Genaro Jr. "Plus, it'll be cool to go to the Island!"

"I like the idea of Padre Island," said Maria Dolores. "It makes me feel very American."

Genaro laughed, as did Toya. "Okay, then. Blackbeard's it is. Vámonos." He twirled the keys and led the way to their van. When he opened the door for Toya, he noticed a little frown on her face. "What's the matter, Vieja? Too much excitement for the little one?"

"I guess so," she replied. "It was just a twinge. It's over. Let's go!"

He started up the van and after a few twists and turns, finally got on Boca Chica Boulevard, which would eventually lead them to Port Isabel, where he could make a right turn and head to the Island. Genaro had always been a very careful driver. When they reached the intersection with Expressway 77, Toya told him to get on it and go straight to Harlingen. "The twinges are five minutes apart now," she said. "I think our little bundle of joy wants to celebrate another way. I'm sorry, everybody."

"What do you mean, you're sorry! This is wonderful! Go faster, Genaro," Maria Dolores was more excited than the parents themselves.

Genaro looked at his wife. "Five minutes apart, did you say? Okay, Let's go!" He turned onto the expressway and sped up, managing to get to Ed Carey Drive in Harlingen within fifteen minutes. By this time, the pains were three minutes apart. He drove to Valley Baptist Hospital and turned into the emergency room. "My wife's in labor. Less than three minutes apart. Call Dr. Rodriguez. NOW!"

Angélica Maria Ruiz Barrios was born thirty minutes later. Now the baby and Maria Dolores would celebrate new life together every year on May 30.

SIX

She heard the sobbing before she actually saw anything; all was blackness around her. She turned toward the sound, and far off, saw her mother kneeling before a coffin. It was gunmetal gray, topped with flowers. The upper half of the lid was open. Marina turned toward her, held out her hand and beckoned to Violet to approach. Violet tried to speak to her mother but no sound would escape. She dragged herself forward. The air was thick, and as she walked, it seemed that she got no nearer to her mother and the coffin. Still her mother beckoned. Still she walked forward. It was Paul in the coffin, she knew that already. Paul, who had been her father, but who had stopped loving her when she was still a child. Paul, who had never ever been satisfied with anything she did.

She felt something fluttering around her ankles and looked down. She was wearing a graduation gown, including the doctoral regalia. And she carried her diploma with her. Her mother motioned once again to join her at the coffin. She looked around, but the pews were completely empty. Where were all the people, she wondered. The chapel had been full when she'd entered the door.

She heard music then, a soft beating of a drum, a faraway flute. The chapel disappeared, but the coffin was still there, and Marina was still beckoning. She had seen the look on her mother's face before. It was love and sadness mixed with regret and pain. She remembered that look from childhood.

She came closer, and saw that an American flag covered the coffin. Her dress had changed too. Now she was wearing Tom's favorite dress, with a shawl around her shoulders. The coffin was no longer gunmetal gray, but pine, plain pine. Under the box, wood had been laid for a funeral pyre. She frowned. Paul would never have wanted this. What must they all be thinking?

Marina turned to her once more. "Oh, Vi, my baby. I never would have wanted this to happen to you." Violet was caught in her mother's embrace, surprised. "He loved you so much. I know he did."

Violet looked into the coffin then. It was not Paul in there. It was Tom, her Tom. She screamed, "No! NOOOO!"

41

April 1981

"No! NOOOO!" Vi thrashed on the bed; her eyes were wide open but she was still clearly asleep. Tom held her and smoothed down her hair, trying to wake her up gently. She was prone to nightmares, sometimes with a bit of ESP thrown in, like when her father died soon after she'd gotten her Master's.

He had promised himself and her then that he would never abandon her, that he would always be there for her. It had been difficult to keep that promise, because their careers sometimes caused them to lead separate lives while linked emotionally and legally. They kept in touch by phone and with weekend getaways while she was working on her doctorate and he was in training.

When she finished her Ph.D. in 1974, she was offered a teaching job at the University of New Mexico; he had been assigned to the field office in Phoenix since '73. They established a home roughly halfway between the two cities, but also kept efficiencies in Albuquerque and Phoenix.

They usually managed to spend three days a week together. Sometimes the days were consecutive, sometimes they were not. They allowed one day for catching each other up on the details of their work. The other two days were given over to doing things they'd always liked to do together: hiking, visiting old people living on the reservations and recording their stories, reading novels to each other, dancing. Last night Felix and his wife had joined them for dinner and dancing.

"What were you dreaming last night, Vi?" he asked her in the morning. They were sitting at the breakfast table, savoring the French toast he'd prepared. "It must have been frightening." He saw the hesitation in her face. "Tell me all about it."

When she finished recounting the dream, he smiled at her and shook his head. "Vi, I've been assigned to our Denver office. I'm not dying, even though it might feel that way. Besides, didn't you tell me last week that you felt like you'd done all you could at UNM? That after eight years, perhaps it was time to move on?" She nodded, blinking back tears. "Well, don't you think this is a perfect opportunity? I mean, Colorado is beautiful country. We could be happy there together. Why don't you look into it?"

"I guess you're right," she responded. "I—I don't know why I let a silly dream scare me so much. Maybe coming up on 34 is affecting me more than I thought it would. Double-three was scary, but going past it is scarier still." They laughed together.

"Well, from where I sit, your thirty-three is not bad, not bad at all!" There was a gleam in his eyes. "Maybe, if you think Colorado is the place for you, we can consider starting a family." She looked startled. "I know we've never talked about it, but hey, I'm going on 40 now. If, and I do mean IF, we're going to have kids, I can't be waiting much longer. But let's think about it for now and talk seriously about it later on, okay?"

She got up to wash the dishes. "It's not that I don't want children," she said. "I've just never thought about it at all. First there was school, then beginning at UNM while you were into your career. I—I guess we should think about it before my biological clock throws me into a panic." She looked at the clock on the wall. "I don't mean to change the subject, but, what's your schedule for today? What time do you have to leave? I have some papers that need grading…care to help me out with them?"

"Hmmm. Let's see. What level are they? Will I be able to grade them, do you think?"

"They're from my intro course. You know the University insists we all teach an intro level at least once a year. Sometimes it's nice to see fresh, young faces excited about anthro. But this semester's class is filled with grazers. You know the type, 'No thanks, I'm just looking.' It makes for difficult teaching, but the papers are easy to grade. It's more like an exercise in beginning composition."

"Well, then Wife, let's get at them! My first appointment tomorrow's at noon, so I don't have to leave before eight. I know you don't have a morning class either, so we can stay here tonight and take off in the morning."

By 3:30 that afternoon, they had graded all the papers, and were in the kitchen having coffee with the pan dulce that Doña Lili had sent them with Felix. The phone rang and Tom picked it up. He grunted a few times into the mouthpiece, then said, "All right. I can be there by seven tonight. Have Elder, Price, and Cañas there at 7:30. I want us to be well-prepared for tomorrow morning." He hung up and looked at Vi. "It seems the President is visiting Phoenix in two weeks. He's been in office two months and already needing to meet with the people. The Secret Service is coming in tomorrow to set up a schedule for the groundwork. Sorry, Hon, but I have to leave now. And I might not be able to make it back before the President's visit"

Vi hugged her husband. "Well, I suppose that'll make us that much happier when we do see each other. I understand, Tom. It's part of your job. I'd rather have this be the President visiting your area than some hostage situation or terrorist threat, honestly. Meetings with the Secret Service don't frighten me as much."

"That's because you've never worked with those guys," Tom laughed. "They really are a scary lot. So, are you staying until tomorrow?"

"Yes. I don't relish going to that little apartment tonight. Call me when you get to the office, okay? I think I'll transcribe some of our interviews with the elders, then perhaps watch television while I do the laundry." She walked him to the door. They both kept enough clothes at both places so that they never had to pack when traveling between work and home.

Vi walked back into the kitchen and washed the dishes they had just used. She walked into the study and took out the cassettes from their last two visits to the reservation. They had spent four hours each visit, talking to the grandparents and great grandparents of life in the old days, and of the stories their elders had told them. Now they had about seventy-five interviews with elders. All were very interesting.

As she worked, Vi developed a kernel of an idea. Perhaps instead of quitting outright, she could ask for a sabbatical from the University. She could live in Denver with Tom and work on a book based on these interviews. That way she could get a sense of whether she would like to spend more time in Denver without making a full commitment to it.

Tom called at 11:30. She told him her idea for the book, and for the sabbatical. He thought it might be a good idea, as long as she didn't go workaholic on him and bury herself in her writing. He knew her well enough to know that was a real danger. They could discover Denver together, he said, and might find that it was a nice place to raise a family if they chose to do so. Much to his surprise, she concurred.

42

May 1987

"Happy Birthday to you, mi Angélica!" Maria Dolores bubbled as she handed a present to her granddaughter. "I made this little gift for you."

"And happy citizenship day to you, Nana," the little girl replied. "You're seven years old as an American too!" She handed Maria Dolores a card she had made for her at school. "My teacher says it is very special that you became a citizen on the day I was born. I told her it was *al revés*, that you became a citizen first and then I was born. Anyway, I made this for you. I hope you like it." Angélica had inherited her mother's talkativeness.

Maria Dolores turned to Toya. "And now you got the job as principal that you wanted. Who would have known. Mija, I'm so proud of you."

"Well, Nana Yolita, we owe it all to you. If you hadn't pushed us, we'd still be renting, living day to day. I give thanks to God every day. But enough of this. I have news. The house is ready. We can move in this weekend if we want. Let's go over to the ranch to see it now. I think you'll really like your room."

They took the back roads to the outskirts of town. Toya drove deftly, as she'd traveled this way many, many times in the past five months. They reached the entry to their property, and she used the remote control to open the gates. Genaro had wanted to add an arch in wrought iron, with the name "Mi Porvenir" written in flowing letters, but she had managed to convince him that it would be too ostentatious. Instead, he had placed a small plaque above the main door to the house. He explained to Toya that he felt it was important to dub it that, because he had worked so hard for it, and because he intended to live and die on that property; it really was his future.

When he started his business, he also started saving for this dream, five percent of net income each month, after paying his bills and his own salary. Sometimes it was only $10, but he always put it aside. When this ten-acre property went up for sale in 1979, he took Victoria to the site and told her about his dream.

Even though they had recently bought a small house, she liked the idea and gave him her full support. He had enough in savings to pay nearly half the asking price; she used her salary to help pay for the rest of it while Genaro continued saving toward the house they would build on it.

Sometimes the two of them would go to the property to daydream. They would talk about the kind of house they would build, what the children would be able to do out there. When the third of their children, Genaro Jr., graduated from high school, they decided it was time to implement their dream. Genaro drew a rough sketch of what they had talked about so many times. When Toya saw it, she suggested a few minor changes, and then Genaro sought out an architect who could turn their ideas into building plans. The dream turned into reality.

A circular drive led up to the house. Toya parked in front, instead of driving to the garages in the rear. The one-story house was imposing. The architect had suggested that a six-bedroom house should have a second floor, but Genaro was adamant that all should be on one floor, and that all the rooms should have at least two entrances.

The architect followed Genaro's instructions to the letter, and the house was a delight to the whole family. It was in the style of a Mexican hacienda, with a central courtyard. A free-form swimming pool dominated the courtyard. The front of the house faced east. The children's bedrooms were in the north and west wings of the house. The master bedroom was in the southwest corner, and Maria Dolores' room sat next to it in the south wing. The west wing housed the laundry/utility room. Behind this was the three-car garage. The kitchen was in the south wing, and the formal dining room took the southeast corner. The living room was next to the dining room along the east face; an entrance foyer separated it from the den.

Maria Dolores exclaimed her delight when she saw the two rocking chairs sitting on the front porch, with a table between them. Toya smiled. "I knew you'd like to sit out here and pray your rosary in the morning. I think maybe I'll join you sometime. Well, let's go on in. I have something special I want to show you."

Maria Dolores wondered at this, for they had all had a hand in decorating the house. Each one had chosen the colors for their rooms. She had even helped select the tiles that were in the kitchen. She followed her daughter to the bedroom that was to be hers. Toya stood at the door, and ushered Maria Dolores inside with a flourish.

Maria Dolores gasped when she saw it. On the far wall, three objects were already up. In the center, a shadow box held her Ojo de Dios, her old and tattered picture of Our Lady of Guadalupe, and an embroidery she had made at least ten years ago, of a mountain with a stream that flowed down to a city…her mountain, a symbol of her early life. On the left, decoupaged on a piece of mesquite wood, the picture of her and Violet at that long-ago kitchen table. They'd had it enlarged. Rose had written "Nana Yolita with Violet" along the bottom. On the right hand side, similarly decoupaged, was a picture of her and Victoria, when Toya was ten years old, right after Maria Dolores had realized the child was her daughter. Rose had written "Nana Yolita with Victoria" on this one. The pictures themselves were framed in roses, pink and yellow and red and lavender. Toya explained that all five of her children had participated in making the gift: Roberto had cut and sanded the mesquite wood. Genaro had the pictures reproduced, and had prepared the shadow box. Rose had done the lettering, and Angélica had found and arranged the roses. Maricruz had done the decoupaging, carefully applying layer after layer until the whole was ready to be displayed.

Maria Dolores was crying. "I cannot believe this! I thought I had lost these when we moved to the other house. Oh, my God. Thank you! Thank you, Virgencita de Guadalupe!" She touched the glass on the shadow box. "Thank you, mijitas!" She hugged both Maricruz and Angélica.

"Nana, don't cry, Nanita!" Angélica hugged her grandmother fiercely. "We only wanted to make you happy. When Maricruz found the Ojo de Dios and your virgencita, she asked us all to help her with the project. We didn't mean to make you sad."

"Oh, no, Angélica, mi angelito de Dios. I am not sad. I am so full of happiness that it just had to spill out in my tears. Because of what you have done, this room is truly mine. Thank you!" Maria Dolores kissed the little girl on the forehead. "But let us see the other rooms now. I am anxious to see what you have done in the rest of the house."

They walked throughout the house, Toya acting as a tour guide of sorts. Angélica's room was the one closest to the master bedroom. She shared a bathroom with Maricruz. The next bedroom was for Genaro Jr., and the one sharing his bathroom was a guest room.

Maria Dolores commented on how big the house was, how difficult it would be to keep it clean. Toya responded with their plan. Each person was responsible for his or her own room, and they would rotate responsibilities for the common rooms. The work list was to be kept in the utility room, so that guests could not readily see and comment upon it. Toya had already made the assignments for the first four weeks, and the lists were on a clipboard in the utility room already. The organization she was known for at school spilled over into her family life.

Victoria winked at her mother, then looked at her watch and exclaimed, "Oh, my goodness! It's two-fifteen already! I have a meeting in fifteen minutes. Nana, Angélica, will you please wait here? I really don't have time to take you home before the meeting."

Maria Dolores smiled at her daughter knowingly. "Of course, Toya. You go ahead. Angélica and I will entertain ourselves here, won't we, mija?" Angélica nodded. "Go on, go on." She shooed Toya away. To Angélica she said, "If I know your father, he already has some sodas in the refrigerator. Why don't we go to the kitchen and see? I don't know about you, but I am thirsty." They padded off to the kitchen after waving Toya off.

Victoria drove straight to their old house, where Maricruz and Genaro Jr. were waiting. They had been preparing party food while Toya had taken her youngest to the new house. Angélica had told them all that just moving to the new house would be celebration enough for her birthday, but they had planned long and hard for this, and this party would go on! Five of Angélica's friends had already been dropped off, and they were waiting for two more. As the parents had dropped kids off, Genaro and Maricruz had given them a map to the new house, inviting them to go from 6—9 PM and join them for a swim and a light supper. Several of the parents had volunteered to bring additional snacks. The birthday party would double as a prelude to the open house/Fourth of July party they would hold in about a month.

As prearranged, Maricruz arrived first, taking along a swimsuit she had bought for her little sister. "Come on, Angie, let's go put on our swimsuits so we can try out the pool! Let's go to Mom & Dad's room; ours still smell like paint." She took her little sister to the bedroom while Toya, Genaro Jr., and Maria Dolores managed to bring in the seven kids and all the party supplies.

By the time Angélica came out again, her friends were standing at poolside, ready to yell "Surprise!"

SEVEN

The *little girl was running as fast as her legs could take her. She was only six years old, but when she saw the green car parked in front of her house she knew it wasn't supposed to be there. Her long black hair was combed in braids, to keep it away from her face, which was blotched from the exertion. The braids trailed behind her as she ran.*

"Nana Yolita!" she cried, tears streaming out of her huge dark eyes. "Nana Yolita, no te vayas...don't go!"

The woman dropped her parcel and ran to meet her, leaving the officers standing beside the car, looking after her. She reached the little girl and swept her up in her arms. "Mi muchachita, mi Violetita...no llores, mi'jita." The woman looked at the men, pleading with her eyes. One looked away; the other, the taller one, merely nodded. She carried the little girl into the house, set her down just inside the screen door, and hugged her tightly. She fell on her knees and took the little girl's face in her hands. Tears were streaming down her dark brown cheeks, forming rivulets of sorrow and pain.

"Los señores son la migra...me tengo que ir con ellos," she explained, as she hugged and kissed the little girl again and again. She took a chain from around her neck, with a medallion of the Virgin of Guadalupe, and put it on the little girl. "Yo te quiero mucho, mi Violetita. No te olvidaré. Stay inside and wait for your mother. Atranca la puerta—lock the door." She waited until the little girl had done so, then she turned

away and walked to the car. The taller of the two men opened the rear door and shut it firmly after her. He could hear the little girl crying and made an effort not to look in her direction. He got in behind the wheel and started the car, taking off without acknowledging the child.

The little girl stood behind the screen door, still crying and screaming, "Nana Yolita!"

43

February 1991

Violet woke up with a start, still crying from the dream. She'd had the same dream for three nights now, and it frightened her more than she cared to admit. It had to mean something, but what? She looked at the clock on her nightstand and saw that it was almost 5:00 a.m.

She decided she wouldn't get any more sleep, so she got up and padded across the white carpet to the bathroom, leaving her brocade slippers tucked neatly under the bed. She brushed her teeth and washed her face mechanically, as she thought about the dream. "Why should I be dreaming of Nana Yolita, after all these years?" she mused. "I'll ask Tom about it when he calls. He'll probably be able to figure it out." Her husband of twenty years, a psychologist with the FBI, was out of town on special assignment.

She was about to get into the shower when her phone rang. She frowned slightly. Who would be calling at this hour? She hesitated a bit, then composed herself. "Hello?"

"Vi? It's your mother, Dear." The voice on the phone sounded broken. Either they had a bad connection, or her mother had been crying. Her mother rarely cried; she was such an optimist.

"Mom? What's wrong? Are you all right?" Violet was instantly alert, fearing the worst.

"It's just a little scare, Dear. I'm in the hospital now. The doctor says I need a pacemaker. I had a bout of indigestion last night that wouldn't go away. Finally I went to a night clinic, and they sent me straight to the hospital. They can't seem to get my heart to hold onto a rhythm. I am 69, you know. So they've scheduled it for tomorrow." Her voice was weak.

Violet slipped into her cool, professional self. "Mother," she said, "I'll be there this afternoon. Is anyone there with you right now?"

"No, Vi. I'm all right. But I look forward to your being with me."

Violet called Tom to let him know about Marina's condition. He asked her to call him when she arrived, and that he would go to Newark on Friday. His work should be finished by then. She told him she would wait to call when she knew anything, and that if he was out she would leave a message at the desk.

She called the airline and made flight arrangements. There was a ten-thirty commuter flight from Dulles that she could take. She'd fly into Newark and could probably be at the hospital by one. She packed quickly, selecting casual clothes that would bear up in the hospital. She called the cab company and arranged for a taxi to pick her up at 8:30. As she reached the door, she turned back and went to her dresser. She opened her jewelry box and picked up the necklace with the gold medallion of Our Lady of Guadalupe and slipped it on. Now she was ready.

Violet reached her mother's room and heard voices inside. They were laughing! She entered and found the nurse taking her vitals. "Mrs. Henderson," the nurse said, "you have such a wonderful attitude! I'm sure you'll do fine with the pacemaker." She turned around and saw Violet. "And you must be her daughter. She described you perfectly!" The nurse extended her arm to shake Vi's hand. "I'm Mrs. Meave, your mother's nurse. Pleased to meet you."

"My mother's nurse?" Vi was a bit confused. "You're a private nurse?"

The nurse smiled. "Oh, no, Mrs. Jackson. Each of the RNs on duty is assigned to five patients during the shift. So, I'm your mother's nurse for this shift. I didn't mean to alarm you. I'll leave the two of you to visit."

Her mother seemed not to have heard what Violet and Mrs. Meave had been saying. "Vi, do you remember Maria Dolores at all? Do you remember what she was like?"

"How strange that you should ask that, Mother. I dreamed about her last night—you know, the nightmare I've had since I was six."

"Yes, I remember your nightmare. But what do you remember about her, about Nana Yolita herself?"

"I remember that she was Mexican. Her skin was very dark and she had eyes that laughed. I used to tell her she had laughing eyes, and she'd pick me up and hug me. She was good to me. She taught me a little bit of Spanish. Her Spanish sounded funny, not quite like the Spanish that our neighbors talked. It had kind of a singsong quality to it that enchanted me." Violet looked as if she were going to say something else, then changed her mind and added, "That's about it."

"Yes, she was Mexican. Mexican Indian. She came to Texas from a small village in Mexico. Somewhere up in the mountains. I never knew exactly where. I guess I never really asked. I wish I had." Marina sat silent for a while before she continued. "Do you remember the little song she used to sing?

Una indita en Xochinacuas
andaba cortando flores
y el indio que la miraba
con sus amores soñaba.
Vestido bonito le voy a comprar,
pa'que se vaya conmigo a pasear.

Such a charming little song." Marina's eyes grew moist again as her voice died down. "She loved you very much, Dear. You know that, don't you? She really loved you very much." She looked to her daughter for a reply.

Violet straightened up, her face unnaturally hard. "She left me. I've been dreaming about that for days. I remember I felt betrayed. Abandoned."

"She was deported, Vi. It's not that she wanted to leave you—us. Somebody reported her and she was deported. She couldn't help it."

"I know that, in my head. But I didn't know it back then. And I was hurt, Mom, so hurt. It was the first of many hurts, I guess. I used to think all the bad things happened because she left. I tried not to blame her, but I couldn't help it."

Marina looked at her daughter with sadness. She knew that Vi was now talking about her father and his rejection of her. That had been so long ago, yet Vi's tone told her it could have been yesterday. If only she'd had the courage then to tell her daughter the whole truth. She'd simply been afraid to lose her. She might lose her still. Yet she had to tell Vi now. Maria Dolores deserved better than a bitter memory.

So she took a deep breath to get hold of herself, and said, "Vi, I'm going to tell you a story. I want you to listen carefully, without interrupting me at all. When I've finished, you can ask all the questions you want. But please, wait until I've finished. It's been inside me for a long, long time, and I want to do it justice. Will you promise me that?"

Violet looked at her mother soberly. She tried to read the expression on her face, but it was impossible. "All right, Mom. I promise." Vi answered.

"When we—Paul and I—were living in Harlingen, I had three miscarriages in as many years. I was nearly thirty years old by then. The doctor told me that I would never be able to carry a baby to term." She took a deep breath.

"How wrong he was, huh?" Vi said quickly, too quickly. Her mother looked at her tenderly.

"Dearest, please, let me finish. I was in the hospital, waiting for your—for Paul to pick me up, and I went to the nursery to have a look…and I saw the most beautiful baby girl. The nurses told me the mother was from Mexico, and was going to be deported, so I talked to her…to Maria Dolores.

"It took some convincing, but she finally agreed to let me adopt you. I promised that she could help raise you, and I kept that promise until the day before your sixth birthday, when the INS picked her up from our house. That same day, your father came home with news of a promotion and transfer to New Mexico. We had two days to make the necessary arrangements, and Maria Dolores had not returned.

"I tried to keep in touch with the neighbors, but they never answered my letters. Later, the summer after you graduated from high school, I even went back to Harlingen, to see if I could find out anything, but by then the neighborhood had changed so much.

"Do you remember how often you asked me what was wrong, when I went to visit you? I was so depressed, because I had finally given up the dream of finding her. Oh, Vi, can you ever forgive me?" Marina broke down, sobbing.

Violet held her mother's hand in silence for a few moments. "Nana Yolita is my birth mother?" Her mind raced, trying to make connections. "Did Paul know? But of course, I'm being silly. He had to know. But I can't imagine it."

"He didn't know, not at first. I—I had lied to him, because I knew of his prejudice against Mexicans. And I wanted you so much. I felt that we were destined to be together," she said between sobs. "But I told him later, when we were living in New Mexico. You were turning eight, and he had gotten upset because you were inviting Clara and Nancy to your birthday party."

The full import of what Marina was saying hit Violet like a sucker punch to the stomach. "And they were Navajo, and he hated Native Americans, right? So you told him about my true heritage, and suddenly he didn't love me anymore. Oh, Mother! I thought I'd done something to make him hate me. But I hadn't." In a way, it was a relief. It was never her fault. It was Paul, his intolerance, his inability to accept people for what they were. "I hadn't."

Violet thought back to her adolescence, to the years she spent trying to be perfect for her father, trying to regain his love. "I spent most of my youth trying to please him. But no matter what I did, he was always cold, polite, as though I were a stranger." She looked at her mother. "Can you tell me why you stayed with him? Didn't you realize what it was doing to me? How I was feeling?"

"I—I had loved him so much that even finding out about his prejudices hadn't affected my love. I knew how he felt about Mexicans, but I had figured out a truce, a way to live with it. And then, in New Mexico, well, I had no skills, no way to make a living. What would I have done? How would I have raised you?" Marina's eyes filled with tears again. "I tried to make it up to you, for his coldness. I suppose I didn't do as good a job of it as I'd thought."

Vi felt that a burden had left her heart. 'Oh, Mom, if only you'd told me then!" The tears she shed now were tears of release, almost of joy.

Marina had regained her composure by then. "I should have, I know. But somehow, I just couldn't. I thought you'd feel a double loss, losing both your father and your mother. I guess there's no excuse, really. But I did what I thought was right, at the time. Then, after he died, well, you were married, you'd already gotten your Master's, lived away from home. I just couldn't seem to find the right time. And I thought we'd never be able to find her."

Violet stood up then, and walked to the window. "And why is now suddenly the right time? Because of your condition? Mother, do you think it is a comfort to me, to know that Maria Dolores was my birth mother? Do you think I want to lose you twice?" She had turned to face her mother, her tears threatening to spill over. "I don't care who my birth mother was, you are my mother!" She rushed to her mother, who opened her arms to her daughter.

Marina caressed Violet, smoothing Vi's hair, whispering endearments to her daughter. "Oh, my sweet Violet, my dearest daughter. I'm not planning to die anytime soon. But just in case the Lord has other plans for me, I decided to tell you the whole truth." She laughed quietly. "Father Henry said I didn't have to tell you, that my confession was enough to put me right with God, but I felt it was important both for you and for Maria Dolores. In my heart, I feel that we will see her again. Wouldn't that be wonderful, Vi?" Marina closed her eyes, and soon was asleep. She never saw the doubt that skipped across her daughter's face.

Vi slipped out of the room and told the nurse she was stepping outside for a moment, but that she would return in a few minutes. She went downstairs and found a pay phone. A quick call to Tom's hotel let her know that he was not yet in. She left a message for him, telling him that she would spend the night at her mother's house. She asked him please to call her, that she needed to talk to him.

Then she stepped out to an enclosed courtyard and pulled a cigarette out of her purse. She hadn't smoked in four months, but had purchased the pack at the airport in D.C. She had suspected she might find an irresistible urge for one during this trip. She found a bench beside a large ashtray, sat down, and lit the cigarette.

She let her mind drift back to her early childhood in Harlingen, Texas. There weren't any real memories, just images of places and people and events. The only solid memory was the one that had recently become her nightmare. She pushed that aside and frowned slightly as she tried to picture the house they lived in back then.

Yes…she could see the white clapboard, with maroon shutters at the windows. There was lush green grass on either side of the walk up to the front porch. The porch was of deep red…marble? No, concrete. And two big fir trees, one on each side, in front of the porch. "To keep the porch cool…and private," her father would say. "This way, none of the Mexicans can look in, no matter how hard they try!" Then he'd laugh, and she would wonder what he meant by that. She realized then that the things her father said had always perplexed her.

She shuddered involuntarily, then concentrated on the house. There was a driveway, and the garage was set back on the lot. She could see the twin tracks of cement leading from the street to the garage. The street wasn't even paved. They had a big mulberry tree behind the garage. It produced the sweetest white mulberries. She smiled at the memory. She closed her eyes and tried to picture how Nana Yolita would have aged by now. The only image that came to her was Nana Yolita in that green INS car, driving off.

Vi returned to Marina's room thirty minutes later, just as they were bringing in her mother's supper tray. She commented on how appetizing the food looked, to which Marina laughed heartily.

Violet supervised her mother's supper without appearing to. Marina was not really hungry, but she ate everything on her tray, so that her daughter would not worry. Afterward, the two sat quietly and watched the local news. Marina reminded Vi that the surgery was scheduled for 7:00 AM, and that she hoped Vi could be back at the hospital by 6:00, before they took her to the operating room.

Vi's eyes twinkled as she said, "Mother, are you trying to get rid of me?"

"Frankly, Dear, yes. I'm not a kid anymore, and I need my beauty sleep," Marina replied. "But I do want you to get some rest too."

Vi went straight to Marina's home. Marina had moved there after Paul's death. It was smaller than the one they had together, but still afforded her a small garden in which to putter without overburdening her. She had contracts with a yard service that came out monthly and took care of the heavier yard work, and with a house maintenance company that came out twice a year to do seasonal maintenance on the house structure and the air conditioner and furnace.

The phone was ringing as she arrived. It was Tom, and he had good news. He was at Newark International now, and could she come pick him up. She almost hung up before she agreed. She felt renewed, and was glad to be able to tell him what she had learned that day.

As usual after flying, Tom was starving. Vi hadn't felt like eating all day, but now that Tom was here, her appetite woke up too. They stopped at a local restaurant and had the daily special. Vi recounted her tale to Tom, who listened attentively but without comment. The older he got, the less apt he was to make quick judgments, or to give quick comment. He had never done that too much anyway, but now he was even more deliberate in everything he did.

Later, in Marina's house and relaxing to *Canyon Trilogy* on the stereo, Vi leaning back against his shoulder, Tom spoke. "You know, Vi, my Bold Deer, it was always somewhat of a mystery how well you fit in with, and how much you cared about the People. It turns out you are one of us, and have always been.

"You always believed that you had chosen your field in defiance of Paul, that he held such sway over your life that he even determined your career. For that reason, you could not let him rest. It seemed he followed you, disapproving, no matter what you did.

"But in truth, the Great Spirit had been leading you to the People, with pieces of dreams that called to you, that invited you to join the quest for wholeness. That is why you have the career you do; that is why you are Bold Deer." He kissed her deeply, tenderly. "And I am grateful to the Great Spirit for giving me a piece of your life."

Violet slept that night as she hadn't slept in years.

Marina was glad to see Tom with Vi the next morning. They both gave her a blessing as she was taken to the operating room.

As expected, Marina came through the surgery well. Within a week, she told Vi and Tom in no uncertain terms that it was time they went on their way and let her resume her own life.

44

July 1996

The twentieth of July dawned hot and muggy in D.C. Violet woke up with a start, knowing she'd had the dream again. In the five years since she'd learned that Maria Dolores was her birth mother, Vi had considered looking for her, but something seemed to hold her back. She honestly did not know how she would react if she ever did find Nana Yolita. Whenever she thought about it, she felt a cold hardness around her heart and in the pit of her stomach, so she simply put it aside. Her rational mind knew this made no sense. How could she let go of the resentment toward Paul, who knowingly abandoned her, yet feel this stone in her heart toward Nana Yolita, who was taken away through no fault of her own? Still, her feelings were real, and there was nothing she could do about them. But in the last two months, she'd had the dream with increasing frequency. Each time, it seemed she saw the pain on Maria Dolores's face more clearly. Tom insisted that the dreams were preparing her for a face-to-face meeting, and that when it was time, the pain would dissipate, leaving only the love.

She looked at the clock on her nightstand, which read 5:25. It was only 3:25 in Albuquerque, much too early to call Tom. The alarm was set at 5:30, to give her plenty of time for her exercise routine before leaving for work. There was no work today, though, because she was starting her 5-week vacation before going to Mexico to do research on a Native American tribe in the state of Jalisco.

She'd finally gotten the go-ahead from the Smithsonian to prepare an exhibit on the commonalities between Mexican and U.S. tribes. There was so much work to do, and Violet was looking forward to it. But first, a time for much-needed rest and relaxation.

She made a mental review of her plans for the day. First, her exercise routine. Then a trip to the doctor's to get a physical. She wanted to have that out of the way before her two extended trips. After lunch, she'd pack her clothes for the trip to Europe. She would fly to New York first, where her mother would join her for the trip. Three weeks in Germany, visiting relatives on her mother's side. They were gracious hosts, who made sure both got a good balance of rest and excitement. She always returned from there feeling refreshed and ready to work.

Tom would join them there in a week, after his conference in San Francisco. He was starting his sabbatical year so that he could go with her to Mexico.

This evening she planned to stay home, watch Nick at Night—*Bewitched* or *I Love Lucy*, talk to Tom on the phone for at least a good half hour, and go to bed early. Her flight to New York was at 6 a.m., and she had no intention of missing it.

She reached over to turn off the alarm. As she did, her phone rang. She frowned slightly. Who would be calling at this hour? She hesitated a bit, then composed herself. "Hello?"

"Vi? It's your mother, Dear."

"Mom? What's wrong? Are you all right?" Violet was up instantly, remembering the scare she'd gotten five years ago, when Marina had to get the pacemaker.

"Oh, Vi! I've found her! Maria Dolores is in Harlingen, of all places. Pack your bags; we're going to the Valley for a visit."

Violet panicked for a moment, then made an effort to answer. "Mother," she said, "this is July. It's going to be over a hundred degrees in the shade there." Vi thought she might not even want to see Nana Yolita again. "How can you even think of going now? I—I don't think it's a good idea. We can go to Harlingen,…oh…, in December." She just wasn't ready to face her again. Maybe she never would be. "I'll be due for a visit to the States then. Besides, we've made plans. Cousin Marta is expecting us."

But there had been no reasoning with Marina Henderson. Once she made up her mind, nothing would change it. Violet had always found that quality both frustrating and endearing. "I've already called her, and she understands. And I think I understand your reaction, Vi. But it really is time; it's way past time, in fact. We're going to Texas. I've made the flight arrangements. Meet me at the airport at two o'clock. That's when my flight arrives. We'll be on our way to Texas at 3:30." With that, she hung up.

Violet was tempted to call back and try to dissuade her, but that would prove fruitless. Instead, she called D.C. Cabs and asked the dispatcher to send Joe Mendes, the driver she preferred. He always knew exactly how much conversation she could take, and her favorite route through the city to Dulles. Though she and Tom had lived here for eight years, she still took the tourist route, going past all the famous memorials. The sight of them thrilled her each time.

She cut her exercise routine short, took a quick bath, and called the doctor's office at 9 to cancel her appointment, saying she'd reschedule when she returned from Texas. She called Tom to let him know of her change in plans. He was visiting Felix and Doña Lili back in Albuquerque on his way to the conference in San Francisco. He asked her if she wanted him to meet her in Harlingen, but she said it would be better if she and Marina went alone at first. Then he asked her to call him when she arrived, and that perhaps he would meet them there after his conference, if they stayed that long.

Then she set about packing. She selected a casual wardrobe: two cotton shirtdresses, a couple of shorts sets, and her taupe knit tank dress. She thought a bit before including two swimsuits, but threw them in just in case they could get to South Padre Island while they were in Texas. A pair of white pumps, one pair of taupe flats, and some leather sandals completed her packing. Now she could relax, drink some coffee and read the paper until it was time to go.

At 12:30, Violet sat in her living room, waiting for the taxi that would take her to the airport. She stood up, looked in the mirror in the entry hall, and considered herself critically. She was not a bad-looking woman, nearing fifty, yet her hair was still blue-black. Until a month ago, she wore it in a sleek pageboy, every strand in place. But when she got the news about her study, she went out at celebrated with a new layered cut. The bangs had been an afterthought, a rare impulse she'd given in to at her hairdresser's just a couple of weeks ago.

As usual, she was impeccably dressed. Her red and white Carolina Herrera, though casual in style, seemed to be tailored to her figure. The red brought a bloom to her cheeks that flattered her pale complexion. White sandals with a one-inch heel and a white straw purse completed her outfit. She wore the barest hint of makeup, just a little eyeliner, mascara, and blush, with a bit of lipstick. Satisfied with her appearance, she returned to the living room sofa.

The doorbell rang, and Violet opened her door. The driver took her suitcase in hand and walked her to the taxi. It was one of the things Violet liked about Mr. Mendes. He was always very attentive, very polite. He took good care of her. And he had a sense of humor that she could appreciate.

"I was surprised to get the call today, Mrs. Jackson," said the driver. "I was all set to come out here tomorrow morning to pick you up. I hope nothing's wrong?"

"Just an unexpected change in my plans, Mr. Mendes. I'm going to Texas with my mother." Violet tried to sound lighter than she felt.

"Texas! Whereabouts? It's a mighty big state."

"The Valley. You know,"

"The Valley! Hey, that's where I'm from! You know where Weslaco is? My hometown. I go back there about every two years, to see my folks. It's a good place, the Valley. Good people…but no jobs. If there were, I'd move back and raise my kids there. There's nothing like being near family. Life's a lot slower there, but there's still things to do. Who do you have in the Valley? Maybe a boyfriend?" He winked at her slyly. "Mr. Jackson know about him?"

Violet smiled at him. Her colleagues would have been surprised at her acceptance of this familiarity, but it was a running joke between this driver and her. She enjoyed it. "Yes, I've heard that it's a good place, with good people. And no, no boyfriend. You know Tom's the only boyfriend I've ever been interested in." Suddenly she felt nervous. She was going to see her Nana Yolita once again! The cab ride continued in silence, driver and passenger each following a separate train of thought.

By the time she arrived at the airport to meet her mother's plane, she'd collected herself and reassumed her usual cool demeanor. The flight came in, several passengers de-planed, then she boarded the plane. Marina waved when she saw her. Her seat was next to Marina's, and she quickly settled in.

Violet looked closely at her mother. Marina was seventy-five, and still going strong. Her dark brown hair was light brown now, as Marina had followed her hairdresser's advice and gone lighter, and her fair skin had developed enough wrinkles to hint at her age without revealing the whole truth. Vi was always surprised to think of her mother as getting older, because she was so active. She still kept her own house and did some gardening. A devout Catholic, she was active in the Ladies' Guild of her parish and in the Charismatic Renewal. Her eyes were bright with caring and enjoyment of life. A tender look from her could make you feel safe and warm, no matter what your problems. Violet noticed there was something different in those warm hazel eyes today; with disquiet, she realized that her mother had been crying.

"Mother? What's the matter? Are you all right?"

Marina waved away her concern, and explained that she could not believe that they would see Maria Dolores once again. It had been nearly forty-two years.

The flight attendant came by, asking if they needed anything. Violet ordered a whiskey sour for herself and a glass of white wine for her mother. She usually did not drink liquor before six, but this day was an exception. The attendant saw that Marina had been crying, and looked at Vi with a question in her eyes, and Vi shook her head slightly, indicating that they'd be all right.

As soon as they were in the air, Violet turned to her mother and asked, "So, how did you find her, after all these years? I mean, I presume you found her just recently, right?"

"Yes. Funny thing is, I wasn't even looking for her. I—you remember that charismatic conference I went to last month? At Notre Dame?" Vi nodded. "Well, on the last day, I was sitting on a bench, under the trees, when I heard a woman speaking Spanish—the Spanish from the Valley. I took a chance and asked her where she was from, and she said she was from Harlingen. Well, I got into a conversation with her, and somehow I got around to mentioning Maria Dolores, and she knew her! I mean, not well or anything, but she knew who Maria Dolores was. Well, I still couldn't be sure we were talking about the same person, so what I did was give her my name and phone number, and asked her to give it to Maria Dolores. I thought that if it was her, she would contact me."

"And so she did. When?"

"I got a call last night, around eight-thirty. It wasn't Maria Dolores; it was her daughter, Victoria. The woman had given them the message yesterday afternoon, but Maria Dolores had been asleep. So when Victoria finally gave her the message, Maria Dolores asked her to contact me right away. She wanted to know about you, Vi. And I couldn't deny her. I talked to Maria Dolores too. She's learned to speak English…and she's become an American citizen! Do you remember how hard she resisted when I decided she should learn to read Spanish? God bless, she is amazing."

"Wait a minute. Her daughter? I have a half sister? Oh my God, it's almost like one of my childhood fantasies is coming true! You know, the one where I imagined I had a twin sister who would always play with me?"

Marina smiled and nodded. "Victoria is meeting us at the airport. She'll take us directly to their house." Marina sat back and closed her eyes. Though her eyes were still puffy from crying, she looked more relaxed than ever before.

Violet took out her compact and looked in the mirror. She was not given to primping in public, but this was not a normal situation. She fluffed her bangs and wondered what Victoria looked like. Perhaps she looked like Nana Yolita.

45

Victoria stood in front of the old mirror in Mama Maria Dolores's bedroom and fluffed her bangs. Her daughter Angélica had talked her into cutting her hair last week. She'd always worn it long, held back at the nape. But now it was layered and short. It made her look years younger. Nana Yolita was sitting up in bed, waiting. Toya turned to face Maria Dolores. "Nana, do you think we will like each other? I am afraid that she won't like us...I mean, she is a gringa." She shook her head. "But she is my sister too. Ay, Dios, cómo habrá pasado esto? How could this have happened?"

Maria Dolores looked at Toya. "We do not always know the ways of God, Mija. When I was the same age as your Angélica, I would never have dreamed of leaving my village. But I have traveled throughout Mexico and the United States. Not in luxury, of course," she laughed, "but all through the two countries. I have learned two languages in addition to my mother tongue...because Spanish was a new language to me at one time, and now I know English as well. Who would have said? Not Doña Elodia, I know. Not even Padre Santiago. Perhaps my grandfather. And of course, la Virgencita." Maria Dolores closed her eyes and breathed heavily. "And now, Toya, you must go to the airport to pick up your sister and her mother. Marina is a very loving person, una mujer de fe, and she must have passed something on to our daughter." She saw Angélica at the door to her room. "Angélica will stay with me until you return. Verdad, Angélica?"

Angélica looked just like her grandmother. "Sí, Nana. I'll stay right here and you can sing 'Una indita' to me like you used to when I was a baby." She turned to look at her mother. "I'm sure Genaro and Maricruz will come home soon from Edinburg. And Beto and Rose are prob'ly on their way. They want to meet la tía gringa too. So you go on to the airport and pick her up, Mami. Nana and I will be right here when you arrive." Angélica escorted her mother to the door and closed it behind her, then returned to her grandmother's bedroom.

Victoria drove her '96 Aerostar minivan to the airport. She looked back on her life, her upbringing. Her life had not been easy, not by any means. But there had always been plenty of love to go around. Even after her father died, Benita and Nana Yolita had made sure that she and her brothers lacked for nothing. What had Vi's life been like? She tried to imagine the life of a gringa, but she could not. Well, she would soon find out! She parked as close to the terminal entrance as she could, stepped out of the van and locked the door. She whispered a little prayer as she walked into the terminal. At least she didn't have to wonder what Violet looked like.

46

The pilot called the descent to Harlingen, and Vi prepared for landing. Marina was ready, her purse in hand. "Mom, it's going to be a little while yet," she said. We still have to taxi up to the terminal. What if Victoria's late? Do you know what she looks like? Oh, I guess we can page her if necessary." The plane stopped, and they disembarked.

She came off the walkway, scanning the crowd standing there, awaiting loved ones. She did a double take when she saw Victoria. Her knees buckled; a man grabbed her elbow and helped her regain her balance.

Victoria was at her side immediately. "You didn't know? I thought you knew! Here…let's sit down." She led Violet and Marina to the nearest bank of chairs. "I don't know why I thought you knew, but it just never occurred to me that you would not know. But of course, if our mother did not know until months after she met me, why would you know? I should have thought of it last night, when I talked to your mother." She looked at Marina. "I'm sorry; I have not introduced myself. I am Victoria Ruiz Barrios." She intended to shake hands, but Marina put her arms around her in a warm embrace.

They went downstairs to claim the luggage; both women had traveled light and had only one bag each to claim. Victoria helped Marina and Violet carried her own bag. She got in the driver's seat of the van and started the engine. Immediately, she turned the air conditioner on high. "Whew! It's melting-hot, isn't it?" She looked in the rear-view mirror and caught her sister's eyes. They had both insisted that Marina take the front passenger seat. "Well, everybody at home is anxious to meet both of you. Nana Yolita couldn't come because she's had a summer cold and is rather delicate right now. You know, the two of you are sort of a legend in our family. Nana has always told us tales about you. She told us you taught her how to read Spanish, Marina. And Violet, you and I are a lot alike, according to our mother. Except that you loved school, and I hated it. And now I'm a school principal. There's poetic justice somewhere in that, I guess. Oops! I'm talking too much again, aren't I? Well, I've always done that too. We're not too far away now. Oh, I know that you made hotel reservations, but I took the liberty of canceling them. We have two guest rooms at home, since Genaro Jr. moved out. I have five children, and the two oldest Roberto and Rosa, have given me three grandchildren. Genaro Jr. got a doctorate in business administration, and is teaching at the university in Edinburg. He has not gotten married, isn't even thinking of it. Maricruz is working on her Masters in Linguistics at UTPA. She's still living at home, but does have a serious boyfriend, Rick, who's in med school. And Angelica, my youngest, turned fifteen in May. How about you, Violet? Do you have any children?" She made a slight face. "Oh gosh! I don't even know if you're married."

"Yes, I'm married," replied Vi. "But unfortunately, we don't have any children. It wasn't for lack of trying, but I guess it just wasn't in the cards for us. Tom would have been a wonderful father."

Toya noticed the wistful look on her sister's face. "Not to worry. Your nieces and nephews will drive you crazy in a few minutes!" She laughed. "You might be glad you don't have any after a bit. No, I'm just kidding.

I love my children very much. I hope that knowing them will be good for you. Your husband couldn't come with you?"

"Actually, Mother and I were going to Germany, to visit her family, and my husband went to New Mexico, to visit friends. This trip to Harlingen is rather impromptu. My husband is expecting a call from me…" Her voice dwindled off, and she wondered if she sounded too formal.

Marina interjected here. "You said Maria Dolores was ill? Is it serious?"

"No, not really. It was just a summer cold, but she doesn't take care of herself, and was out on the patio, watering the plants. She got her feet wet, and that just made it worse. Last night and this morning she had a little temperature. It was gone by this afternoon, but we didn't want to take any chances. Angélica decided she should stay in bed, and has been 'babysitting' her since noon. She is very attached to her grandmother. She might be only fifteen, but she's very strong. She will be a woman to be reckoned with. Probably more so than either of her older sisters. Here we are." She pressed the gate opener, which also rang a bell inside the house.

Genaro, Genaro Jr., and Maricruz were waiting on the porch as they drove up. Genaro opened the van doors and welcomed the visitors. He asked his son to take their bags to the rooms that were prepared for them, and asked if they wanted to go to their rooms before going in to see Nana Yolita.

The two women spoke in unison. "No, I'd like to see her, please." They looked at each other and smiled. Marina asked Vi if she minded her being there the first time she saw her mother. Vi told her she would prefer it. They followed Victoria through the courtyard to Maria Dolores's room.

47

Maria Dolores heard them coming, and stepped out to the courtyard to meet them. She was crying before they got close. "Marina! Mi Violeta! Oh, how I have longed for this day!" She opened her arms to heaven. "Thank you, Virgen de Guadalupe, for bringing my family together. Thank you, Tata Dios, for the love and care you have for me."

Marina looked at her friend with a measure of astonishment and pride. Maria Dolores had been so shy, so scared when they had first met. She had grown in confidence in the six years they'd lived together, but nothing like what she was seeing now. Her black hair, once worn in braids, was now gathered into a sophisticated bun at the nape. The highlights still shone blue-black in the sun.

"Maria Dolores, look at you!" she exclaimed. "Oh, my friend, it is wonderful to see you. I thank God too, for that chance encounter at Notre Dame, that brought renewed hope of seeing you." She hugged Maria Dolores, and the two women sat down together on the wicker love seat under the potted palms.

Marina's actions gave Violet a chance to look closely at Maria Dolores.

She was so much smaller than Vi remembered! She had to be less than five feet tall. And Vi knew for certain now where her fascination with high cheekbones originated. But what held the greatest impact were her birth mother's eyes and smile. They radiated such love, such warmth. This love had been missing in her life all these years. She felt the years fall off her spirit. "Nana Yolita, yo ti quero!" she cried out, reverting to the language in which Maria Dolores had spoken to her. She ran to the two women and knelt in front of them. Both of her mothers embraced her. They stayed like that for several minutes, then all three stood up and were embracing each other, trying to make up for the years together that they had lost. Marina stepped aside and let Maria Dolores and Vi have some time to themselves. She watched as Maria Dolores touched her daughter's face, wiping away the tears that had sprung from Violet's eyes. All the while, Maria Dolores was muttering in three languages, "Noconeuh. Mi niña. My daughter. Gracias, Virgencita. Notlazocamai, Cihuapili. Thank you, Lady."

The Barrios family had left them alone in the courtyard when Maria Dolores had stepped out from her room. Now, the youngest came out with a tray of iced tea for them. She approached Violet. "Tía Violeta, I am Angélica, the youngest of your nieces and nephews. But not the youngest of your relatives, because my oldest brother Robert has a nine-month-old son." She looked at Vi almost shyly. "Would you like some tea? It's very hot out here. Or maybe all of you would like to come into the den? Oh, I don't mean to intrude, but I was just so curious to meet my aunt. You see, all of my other aunts, from my dad's side, they're in California, and we only see them, like, maybe once every two or three years, if that. So we don't really get to know them all that much. But I think we'll spend more time with you." By this time she had set the tray on the table. She covered her mouth with her hands, then continued. "Not that I mean you have to, like, stay with us for a long, long time. It's just that I hope, oh, I don't know, I hope that we'll get to really know you, you know? And I...." She paused, took a deep breath, and looked at her grandmother. "I'm running off at the mouth again, aren't I?"

Vi embraced the young girl. "You know what, I used to talk a mile a minute too, when I was small. People used to say I should become a lawyer, I talked so much."

Angélica laughed. "That's what my brothers and sisters tell me, too! But I don't want to be a lawyer. I want to take over my dad's business when I am able. I think he's a wonderful man. What's your husband like? Mom tells me you're married, but don't have any children. That's okay. I don't think every woman has to have children to be fulfilled. But it means I get to spoil you as my aunt. I'll give you lots of love, and I'll tell you all my troubles, and we'll have a wonderful time together. Tell me that you think it's a good idea."

Victoria walked into the patio with a tray of vegetables and dips. "Angélica, leave my sister in peace! She just got here. Besides, I haven't had a chance with her yet. We're identical twins, you know. I have to find out for myself if what they say about twins is true." She turned to address Violet. "Don't you think it's funny, that both our first names should begin with V? I mean, I know that Nana Yolita gave you your name. But she didn't give me mine. My mother Benita named me after her mother. Also, how long have you worn bangs?"

Vi answered, "Two weeks. How about you?"

"Two weeks," Victoria replied. "Do you think it's just coincidence?" The sisters laughed together. "In college, what did you major and minor in?"

"My major was anthropology. I minored in English," Violet said. "What about you?"

"Majored in English, minored in sociology...there was no anthropology minor at Pan Am, or I would have chosen it." Maria Dolores and Marina had stopped talking to each other, and were watching the two sisters bond. Both older women still had tears in their eyes. In fact, the entire family watched in amazement as the two sisters made similar gestures in response to certain triggers: both played with their necklaces, both bit their lower lips before breaking out in a smile, and both habitually pushed the hair on the right behind the ear.

Genaro interrupted them. "I know you two have lost all track of time and space, but the rest of us are hungry. The pizzas are here. I ordered salads for all of us, too. One large pepperoni, one Canadian bacon and mushroom, and one large Veggie pizza for Toya."

"And for Violet," Marina added. Victoria and Vi laughed together.

"Even your laugh sounds the same!" said Robert. He extended his hand to Violet. "I'm the older son, Robert. And this is my wife, Marta, and our two kids, Bobby and Olivia."

Rose approached Vi and Marina. "I'm Rose, my husband Jesse. And my son, Jesse Jr."

They all ate, sampling each pizza, joking and laughing. As they were finishing, the phone rang. Angelica ran to answer it. "It's for you, Tía! I think it's my uncle….he has such a dreamy voice!"

Vi took the phone from her niece. "Tom? Oh, Hon, I'm sorry I didn't call you earlier! I—We just got carried away."

"Well, I'm really glad to hear things are going well for you. I was just worried when I called the hotel and found your reservations had been canceled. Actually, the hotel clerk helped me out. It seems he had been a student of your sister's, and he gave me her husband's name. From there, information gave me the number." Tom sounded a little annoyed.

"Tom? You have to come, meet my family. We've only just met, but it feels like I've known them all my life. Victoria and I are identical twins. It's almost spooky, but it feels so good. Will you come?"

"I've already made flight arrangements for Saturday—that's day after tomorrow. I thought a couple of days alone with your family would be good for you. I can hardly wait. Oh—Felix said it was just my luck to have two mothers-in-law. He says hello, and congratulations on finding your birth mother. Hon, I think I'll let you go back to the family. Felix and Betty are waiting for me; we're going to El Nopal for dinner, then they'll put me on the plane for San Francisco. My presentation is on Friday afternoon, so I'll be free Saturday morning. My flight gets into Harlingen at 1:45. I presume you'll pick me up?"

"Of course, Darling! Probably Toya and I will both be there. See you then. Give my regards to Felix, Betty, and Doña Lili. And Tom? I love you. More than I can say."

"I love you too, Vi. More than you can know," Tom answered. It was their usual long-distance sign-off, started back when Vi went to grad school in Toronto.

When Tom arrived on Saturday, he fell right in with the family. He and Genaro shared more than one joke on the idiosyncrasies common to their wives, until both sisters had enough and told them to "stop it right now this instant!" Hearing that phrase in stereo pushed both husbands into paroxysms of laughter.

Violet and Victoria seemed determined to make up for all the years they had spent apart. After Mass on Sunday, they left their husbands by the pool at home and took off to Nuevo Progreso together. "It's much smaller than either Matamoros or Reynosa, and the shopping is fine," Toya explained to her sister. "I know a place where we can get pedicures for less than $10.00!" That evening, they came back sporting red toenails and white embroidered peasant dresses. The husbands immediately offered to make margaritas and put on mariachi music for their beautiful "señoritas." The wives giggled at this and as demurely as possible accepted the invitation. Tom looked at his wife from the kitchen and said to Genaro, "I don't think I've ever heard Vi giggle before. It's a wondrous thing."

Genaro laughed, "Well, concuño, get used to it. I love to hear my Toya giggle. That's one of the things that kept me going when times were tough for us. Here, you take the chips and salsa, I'll carry the 'Ritas." They rejoined the women in the courtyard.

"Where are the abuelitas and Angélica?" Toya wondered aloud.

"Well, Marina mentioned that she hadn't been in Harlingen in such a long time and would like to see some of the old neighborhoods. Angélica volunteered to be navigator, and I gave them the keys to my truck."

Vi nearly choked. "Mom is driving your 4 x 4? I can't believe it!"

"Wait till you see her! She had to put one of the throw pillows from the sofa behind her back," laughed Genaro. "She really is something else! It didn't even faze her a bit."

The music changed from mariachis to trios, and Genaro put down his glass. "Come on, Vieja. Let's dance." He turned to Tom, "Andale, Tom, vamos a bailar todos."

Vi was about to protest when Tom said, "Vi, may I have the honor of this dance?" She nodded silently. They hadn't danced together since the miscarriage fifteen years ago. She had not felt like it at first; finally he had simply stopped asking. She took his hand and went into his arms. He led her in the one-two-three step of the bolero that he had taught her to dance when they were first dating, so many years ago.

Marina, Maria Dolores, and Angélica walked in as the music ended. They applauded and the two couples bowed. They had several bags with them, and Angélica gave one to each person. "I hope you're all ready to head out to the beach tomorrow! Remember, we have the condo this week, Mom!" Toya nodded. "Oh, and I got each of you a present. Look in the bags." The sisters found identical swimsuits. They looked at Angélica with a question. She shrugged, "I figured y'all didn't get to do the 'twin-thing' when you were little, so…" She turned to the men, who looked into their bags and started laughing. They pulled out t-shirts that said, "I'm with the **beautiful** twin."

Victoria went back to work on the first of August, and Vi, Tom, and Marina would spend hours talking with Maria Dolores. One day, Tom went to Nana Yolita's bedroom to look for her, and he noticed the plaques and the shadow box on the wall. He looked at the embroidery in the shadow box; it looked familiar. It took but a few seconds to see the similarity to Felix's portrait of them.

Maria Dolores walked in and said, "That is what I remember of my mountain home, back in Mexico. It was so beautiful there, Tom. The river that went by our village, it sounded so—soothing is the word, I think. You could not stay troubled in spirit when you sat by that river. And there was always birdsong. My grandfather, the father of my mother, used to say that the songs of the birds carried away our fears and planted instead dreams of the eternal. Sometimes I wake up with small pieces of those dreams in my mind. I spent less than fifteen summers on that mountain, but they have guided the fifty since I left there." She walked to the window and stood looking out. "Sometimes I dream of that mountain, and of my grandfather, and of my husband. We were married less than four months before the plague took him, but I never could imagine loving another man. Victoria is like that, and so is Violet. I am glad that she chose well in marrying you, Tom. I am glad that you understand her." She took his hand and kissed it. He had tears in his eyes as he knelt in front of her, took both of her hands in his and kissed them.

In the evenings, the two sisters spent time alone with each other. Violet cried with Victoria over all her losses, her father, her brothers, her mother Benita. Victoria ached with Vi over the pain of her father's rejection. They cried together with a mix of pain and joy that Nana Yolita had never even contemplated aborting them, though they were the product of a rape.

Two nights before Vi, Tom, and Marina were scheduled to leave, Victoria spoke with her sister. "I have never spoken of many of these things with anybody, not even Genaro. The few times I tried to talk to Nana Yolita, she told me, 'If you walk backwards, you will surely stumble and fall.' I asked her what that meant, and she said, 'My Tata Diego told me I must always go forward, never back. If I look too much at the things that happened and think them bad, then I will fall over the good things, never knowing how good they were. You and Violeta are good, Victoria. We must not taint your goodness.' So I never asked her again about the circumstances of our conception. But I knew it couldn't be good. When Marina told me of the rape, I understood so much." She sighed deeply. "Vi, I don't want to lose you. You're going back to Washington, then to Mexico for your project." Her eyes glistened with unshed tears. "There is still so much to learn from each other. When will I see you again?"

"I've been thinking about that, too. I really do have to finish this project I've started. I mean, it's something I've been working for practically all of my adult life. Let's see—I'm spending about four or four and a half months in Mexico, then it'll take another three or four to mount the exhibit. Tom and I could come by here around Christmas or so? And then maybe you and your family could come up to DC for spring break? I'd really love to show you the capital, Toya. How about that? Is it a deal?"

"It's a deal!" Victoria replied, hugging her sister.

On Saturday morning the whole family went to the airport to see them off. Angelica and Maricruz surprised them with a family album that included pictures of each family member, from Genaro to Angelica, and also pictures of Benita and Marina side by side. Finally, they had added pictures taken during the stay. Vi couldn't believe her eyes when she saw hers…and then they gave an identical album to Marina. It was very touching. She hugged each of her relatives, whispering her love. When she came to Maria Dolores, her mother kissed her tenderly, and blessed her, making the sign of the cross as she said, "In the name of the Father and of the Son and of the Holy Spirit. May God bless you and the Virgencita de Guadalupe accompany you in your journey and in all that you do. Mi Violetita, I am at peace, because I know you are well and in good hands." Violet felt a tiny flutter in her breast as Nana Yolita blessed her.

Nana Yolita turned to Tom and blessed him too. "Ximopanolti," she added. "It is Nahuatl for 'Go safely.' But to me, it means much more. It means that the past is past, it is done. It means go forward, because Toteotzin and Cihuapili are with you. No matter what bad things happen, you are safe, because they bless you. You, Tom, are a blessed one."

Their flight was not crowded; there were only three other passengers in first class. Tom and Vi sat together, and she worried a bit about her mother. But when she looked over, Marina was already engaged in a lively conversation with her seating partner. Both seemed to be enjoying it.

Tom commented on her family, how they had accepted him, how comfortable he felt with them. "And Nana Yolita, what a delightful woman! I can see where you get your own determination and spirituality, Vi."

Vi looked at him. "Spirituality?" she questioned. "I've never considered myself particularly religious. Mother was," she nodded toward Marina. "But after Paul put that barrier between us, I guess I got mad at God or something. I mean, I'd go to mass with Mom, but I spent the whole time arguing at Him."

"Well, that's precisely what I mean. You might have been angry with God, but you still believed. And besides, I didn't say religiosity. I said spirituality. You have a reverence for life in all forms that is deeply spiritual. And I do remember catching you at prayer a time or two. Maybe not formal prayer, but prayer nonetheless. Or are you going to deny it?" Tom's eyes twinkled

She smiled. "To tell the truth, there have been times when I didn't think I would have made it without God's help. Like the months we were apart while I was in grad school. Or that time that you were shot and I didn't even know where you were, I just got a call saying that you had come through the surgery just fine and that they would let you come home as soon as you were able. And especially back in '81 when we finally decided to get pregnant, and then I miscarried. Our daughter would be almost Angelica's age now. And when the doctor told us I'd never be able to have a baby. And Mother's heart surgery five years ago. Tom, I don't know what I would have done without God's help." She took his hand. "All these years, God has taken care of me—of us."

Tom added, "And so has, according to Nana Yolita, the Virgin of Guadalupe. Let's not forget her. What does she call her?" He thought a bit. "Ah, yes. Cihuapili. The Lady."

Tom closed his eyes and soon was asleep. Vi smiled and brushed back a lock of hair that had fallen into his eyes.

EIGHT

The old man hurried down the mountain path. He looked down to the base of the mountain anxiously, as if looking for something. He stopped and cocked his ear, as if listening to something.

The Turquoise Lady came to his side and smiled. He looked into her eyes, then looked down the path, as if asking her a question. She nodded slightly, and then both of them walked down together. As they walked down the path, the mountain air filled with the scent and color of roses. Birdsong accompanied them.

The old man saw, far down the path, someone dressed in pale blue. His heart quickened, and so did his pace. He reached his granddaughter and embraced her. She looked at him in wonderment and touched his face, kissed his hands. Then she looked down the mountain again.

By this time, the Lady had reached them. She pointed to the granddaughter's left hand, and for the first time the granddaughter realized it was clenched. She opened it and saw a small mound of pebbles. The Lady motioned for her to set them down, and let them roll. She did so, whispering, "Ximopanolti. Go safely."

She quickly turned back to her grandfather and to the Lady.

Hand in hand, they walked home, reveling in the sights and sounds that greeted them.

The brightness that surrounded them released a little piece of itself, which drifted to the pebbles and dropped over them in a gentle rain.

Printed in the United States
75023LV00004B/1-99